BOUND BY DESIRE

ALSO BY JAYMIE HOLLAND

Taken by Passion
Claimed by Pleasure

BOUND BY DESIRE

JAYMIE HOLLAND

St. Martin's Griffin
New York

Roy Holland

This is a work of fiction. All of the characters, organizations, and events portrayed in this novel are either products of the author's imagination or are used fictitiously.

www.stmartins.com

Design by Anna Gorovoy

Library of Congress Cataloging-in-Publication Data

Holland, Jaymie.
    Bound by desire / Jaymie Holland. — 1st ed.
        p. cm.
    ISBN 978-0-312-38665-8 (trade pbk.)
    1. Shapeshifting—Fiction.   I. Title.
    PS3613.C38634B68 2012
    813'.6—dc23

                                            2011041082

First published in the United States in e-book format under the title Wonderland: *King of Diamonds* by Ellora's Cave Publishing, Inc.

First St. Martin's Griffin Edition: March 2012

10 9 8 7 6 5 4 3 2 1

AUTHOR'S NOTE

I hope you enjoy *Bound by Desire,* where futures haven't yet been painted.

Cheyenne McCray
aka Jaymie Holland

BOUND BY DESIRE

PROLOGUE

THE MANSION'S WINDOWPANES RATTLED AND thunder cleaved the night as a brilliant flash of lightning briefly illuminated the dim room. Smells of burning tallow, sandalwood, spice, and scents of arousal from the two women in his bedchambers caused Karn's nostrils to flare and his cock to stiffen.

Like a caged tiger, the Ruler of the Kingdom of Diamonds paced his expansive candlelit chambers and ignored the two naked females silently waiting for him. Cool air caressed his scarred chest, and he flexed his muscles as he fought against what he was required to do. For even though he was king of his own realm, he still answered to the High King, his brother Jarronn.

Unlike his three brothers' castles and palaces, Karn resided in a stately mansion. He preferred to live in a home that was elegant, yet understated. The endless moors around his manse gave him comfort and a sense of peace. His subjects within the Kingdom of Diamonds were loyal to Karn as well as to Jarronn the High King of Tarok.

He paused before one window and looked out into the darkness. The storm obscured his view of the village, the surrounding homes, and even the ocean, giving the dark mansion a feeling of being more remote than it actually was.

Lost in his thoughts, Karn barely spared a glance at the two cards lying facedown upon the *a'bin*. Despite his orders, despite the sorceress Kalina's urgent plea that he choose a card and select his mate as his elder twin brothers had, Karn was loathe to comply. He had no desire to bring a woman from another world into a loveless joining . . . for Karn would never love anyone outside his brothers and their mates, his nieces, and his nephews. Even to those individuals, a portion of his heart was cut off and would be known to none.

Not after losing his parents to a magical fever, not after losing his sister to evil insanity, not after losing the one woman he had ever given his love to.

No. He would never love again.

Instead of the magical cards, Karn stopped pacing and focused his attention on Kalina and Aleana, his favored pleasure toys. Flickering candle flame danced upon the midnight-dark skin of Aleana who stood beside the *a'bin,* at the foot of his massive four-poster bed. Her dark skin was perfection, like silk made from the night sky and created for a man's touch. A single white lock graced her long black hair, framing one side of her face as it spilled from her part, over her forehead, and down to her shoulders. The paleness of the lock was a stunning contrast to her lovely skin.

"My beauty." Karn moved close enough to Aleana to lightly stroke her breasts with his fingertips. He pinched one pierced nipple and she gave an excited cry. The white diamond hanging from the piercing glittered in the candlelight, casting rainbows throughout the dim room. "Do you know what I desire of you, my sweet?" he asked.

Aleana licked her full burgundy lips with the tip of her tongue, her brown eyes flashing with need. "I wish only for your pleasure, Sire."

With a nod, Karn motioned to Kalina to come closer as he continued to fondle Aleana's nipple. "Before I perform my duty to my people, I wish for you to perform your duty to me," Karn said.

Thunder rumbled again as the sorceress approached and he could feel the charge in the air as the sky prepared to break loose with all its fury.

When Kalina was close enough, Karn reached out and rubbed the pad of his thumb over her taut nipple and its diamond piercing, causing her to gasp with pleasure. "You have little time, Sire. The path will not stay open for long."

"I am aware of how much time I have and do not have." Karn's voice held just enough reproach that Kalina lowered her fire-ice eyes.

"Yes, Sire."

He let his hands fall away from the women and stepped back so that he might better observe his pleasure toys. "Sorceress, I wish for you to suck Aleana's nipples."

Kalina's expression was one of desire as she turned to Aleana. The sorceress cupped the woman's breast, lowered her head, and flicked her tongue across Aleana's nipple as instructed.

Aleana moaned and arched her back, forcing her nipple farther into Kalina's mouth and the sorceress sucked harder yet. Kalina brought her hands to Aleana's slender hips as her mouth moved to the woman's other breast.

Karn's cock stiffened at the sight of Kalina's ivory flesh against Aleana's ebony skin. It never ceased to please him to watch two women pleasuring each other and then to fuck them both until they could take no more. However, he had yet to discover a partner with whom he could find complete release, and now that he was forced to choose his queen from a card, he likely never would. Even two women fully trained in sexual arts could not satisfy him. How could one woman do so— and a woman ignorant to the sensual ways of his own world, no less?

A flash of light and then thunder boomed again. "Widen your stance, Aleana," he commanded as he slowly walked around the two women, enjoying the sight of their naked bodies. When Aleana obeyed, he stopped behind Kalina, grabbed a handful of the sorceress's black hair as she liked him to, and pulled downward. "Lick Aleana's quim."

"Yes, Sire." Gracefully, Kalina knelt, her mouth curving into a sensual smile, and Karn released his hold on her. She used her slender fingers to part Aleana's slit.

Kalina flicked her tongue against the woman's clit then buried her face within Aleana's folds.

Aleana moaned and slid her hands into Kalina's hair, pressing the sorceress even tighter against her quim.

A low rumble rose up in Karn's chest and moved into a loud purr as he watched his lovely playthings. His lust always raged at the sight of them teasing each other. He enjoyed watching a woman reach climax. Even better was seeing two women orgasm at once.

"May I come, Sire?" Aleana asked, her brown eyes meeting his gaze.

"Not yet." He gestured to the black hide on the dark flagstone floor, beside the sorceress's *a'bin*. "Kalina, cease. Go, and lie on your back upon the bearskin."

The sorceress lifted her head, licked Aleana's juices from her lips, and hurried to do as he bade. She settled on the coarse rug, looking both relaxed and excited. Ah, but she was beautiful, her flawless skin so white against the black fur.

"On your hands and knees over Kalina," he ordered Aleana. "And make sure your breasts are above the sorceress's mouth."

"Yes, Sire," Aleana replied as she obeyed.

"Kalina, I wish for you to suck Aleana's nipples while I fuck her."

"Yes, Sire." Kalina grasped both Aleana's breasts in her hands and held them so that the woman's nipples were close enough together that both could easily be stroked with her tongue.

Karn knelt behind Aleana, between Kalina's wide-spread thighs. Aleana moaned as he caressed her gorgeous firm ass and as Kalina sucked her nipples. He enjoyed viewing a woman's quim from this angle, and with the sorceress beneath Aleana, he had a fine view of her lovely folds as well.

With his magic he summoned a three-dimensional diamond-shaped toy that he often used with his beautiful playthings. As he placed the head of his cock to Aleana's core, he put the toy to Kalina's quim.

"What would you like me to do to you?" Karn asked as he fondled Aleana's ass.

"If it pleases you, Sire," Aleana said in a voice that told him she found it difficult to speak, "I wish for you to fuck me."

"That's my sweet." Karn teased her opening for a few seconds, just long enough to make her groan with anticipation. Then, as he drove his cock into Aleana, he slipped the toy into Kalina.

Both women shouted and moaned. With his free hand, he spanked Aleana's ass the way he knew she enjoyed it, the sound of each slap ringing out in the room and mingling with the crash of thunder. She gave cries of delight and thrust back against him; at the same time, he pushed into her and spanked her.

He watched his cock moving in and out of her and his lust increased, yet he would not allow himself to reach his peak.

It was only moments more before Aleana begged him again to let her climax. When he gave her permission, she immediately cried out and her core contracted around his cock. She was still recovering from her orgasm when he ordered her to move so that she was to Kalina's side.

He was kneeling between only Kalina's thighs then. Long had he enjoyed fucking the sorceress the times he visited the Kingdom of Hearts when she served his brother Jarronn, and later in Spades when she belonged to Darronn. Now she was Karn's . . . until he took his own queen, and she would then go to the youngest king, Ty.

Karn pulled the diamond-shaped toy from Kalina's quim and used his magic to send it back to its place in his room. The sorceress's eyes were heavy-lidded with lust as he hooked his arms beneath her knees and brought her ass up high enough off the floor so that she was at the perfect level for his cock.

"Lick Kalina's clit," he ordered Aleana, and she quickly complied.

Aleana knelt on the bearskin and lowered her face to the sorceress's clit, while Karn drove into Kalina's core. She moaned and fondled her own nipples as Aleana licked her folds and Karn fucked her.

"May I come, Sire?" the sorceress begged, but he refused her.

While he thrust in and out of Kalina, he released one of her legs to reach over to the *a'bin* and hold his hands above the two cards. The second one glowed and a jolt of sensation ran through his body and straight to his cock, so intense he almost came.

Karn snatched the card up, even as he continued to

fuck the sorceress. And then he almost lost control yet again as he turned the card over and for the first time saw his future mate.

Annie. The name came to him like a whisper on the wind. *Her name is Annie.*

Long brown hair, a voluptuous body, and beguiling innocence wrapped in one delectable package. Suddenly, it was Annie he imagined he was fucking. It was the woman in the card who enjoyed the combined pleasures of Aleana's tongue and his cock.

"May I come, Sire?" he heard the desperate plea from far away.

Yes, kitten, he responded to the woman in the card. She whimpered and came, her core milking his cock. His own orgasm slammed into him and he growled as he emptied his fluid into her quim.

Slowly he returned to the present, the card still in his hand and the sorceress and Aleana before him.

Not the woman from the card.

The shock of being transported from the moment of imagining he was fucking his future mate made him nearly speechless.

He withdrew from the sorceress. Her pleased and well-sated expression told him that not only had she experienced pleasure at his hands, but that she had seen him take the card and was satisfied with his response.

Karn felt a mixture of irritation and intrigue. He hadn't expected anything, much less such a strong wave of sensation. He stood, moved to the window, and gazed out into the stormy night. Lightning illuminated his realm, a land slipping into spring. Thunder boomed and windowpanes rattled again.

"It is time," he murmured under his breath. "It is time."

CHAPTER ONE

ANNIE TRAVIS SQUEEZED A DAB OF NAVY-BLUE paint onto her palette, her hand trembling slightly as memories of the past two years threatened her creative energy. First, her cousin Alice had disappeared and then exactly a year later to the day, Alice's twin, Alexi, vanished.

The note. Remember the note, Annie reminded herself as she screwed on the tube's lid and put the paint back into her artist's toolbox. The room smelled of her paints and of the unlit cranberry and spice candles in her apartment. Her cat, Abracadabra, curled around Annie's ankles and warmed her bare feet.

She tossed her braid over her shoulder and stared at the enormous blank canvas that was four feet high and three feet wide. She had no idea why she'd purchased one this size; it was certainly too big for her apartment. Perhaps it would look good in Aunt Awai's condo, depending on what scene Annie came up with. Something was stirring in the back of her consciousness. It was as if her mind was already working on what she wanted to paint, and she just needed to give it a little more time to gel.

Abra gave a little "*Meow*," as if reminding Annie she was supposed to be painting and not moping over her missing cousins. Annie absently reached down from her stool to rub behind the calico cat's ears until Abra purred and nuzzled Annie's bare feet.

With a smile, Annie pushed her wire-rimmed half-glasses up the bridge of her nose, then selected a paint-brush with heavy bristles. For a moment, she glanced away from her canvas to the window. The curtains were tied back so that she could clearly see the rare sunny morning, the sky a cerulean blue with just a few wisps of transparent clouds streaking the horizon.

She lived with only Abra for company, right off the beach in Pacifica, a suburb of San Francisco. Year-round, the Pacific Ocean in the Bay Area was too darn cold for anyone to brave it without wetsuits, but Annie wasn't much into water sports anyway. She'd chosen the apartment because rent was cheaper here than in the city, and because she loved to watch and to *experience* the ocean, with all of her artist's senses. The dark push and pull of the waves, the way they crested pearl-white when the water was rough and slammed onto the beach, the stark black cliffs against slate blue waters, and the tang of salt and brine in the air.

But today she was attempting to portray the sunny

beauty outside and get her mind off of her missing twin cousins.

Yellow. Bright, happy, relaxing . . . It's not working.

A few months after Alexi's disappearance, Annie had gone to the twins' town house to clean it out for the landlord and to put her cousins' belongings into storage. But when she'd walked into Alexi's bedroom, she found a rolled-up piece of parchment tied with a black ribbon on Alexi's bedspread. A spade crest was stamped onto a wax seal.

After Annie had removed the tie, broken the seal, and unrolled the note, she saw that it was written in Alexi's bold scrawl. It even looked as if she had used a quill, of all things—there were a couple of smudges and a blob of ink at one corner.

A kaleidoscope of emotions had whirled through Annie when she'd first read the note. Uncertainty, disbelief . . . and hope. Definitely hope.

Dragging herself back to the present, Annie set her paintbrush onto her easel and slipped one hand into the pocket of her smock to retrieve the parchment. She didn't know why she'd taken it from her nightstand this morning. Maybe it was for the comfort it gave her to read the words she was sure Alexi had penned. It was as if her cousin was talking to her, reassuring her.

Annie's hands were steadier now as she slipped the black tie from around the note and let the ribbon fall to the floor. The parchment felt thick and coarse to her fingertips as she smoothed it out on her lap and read it for at least the hundredth time.

Dear Annie and Aunt Awai,

Please don't worry about Alice and me. It's a very long story, and it's one I hope to tell you one day in person. But for now just know we're both safe, and we're both happy. It's likely we won't be able to see you until another "path" opens between us. I know this all sounds cryptic, but please trust me.

So that you'll know it's me and not someone else: Annie, remember the time Alice and I accidentally turned your hair orange when we were teenagers? We were grounded most of our eighth-grade year over that one. Never thought you'd forgive us.

And Awai, I bet you'll never forget the time we broke that unusual glass cylindrical sculpture we found in your bedroom. Of course, it wasn't until a couple of years ago that I ran across one in an erotic boutique and learned it was a glass cock. Go, Auntie!

Hugs and kisses from both Alice and me. I found her! Well, more or less. Anyway, you can imagine how happy I am. I only wish that you could be here with us.

I also wish they had computers here, and e-mail. This ink stick is frickin' hard to write with.

All my love, Alexi

A smile tugged at the corner of Annie's mouth, while at the same time tears burned behind her eyes. Amused and sad—the two emotions blended like discordant colors. She shook her head as she retrieved the black ribbon from Abra who had pounced on it when it fell on the floor, and promptly attacked it.

"Listen, you little imp," Annie said as she leaned down and snatched up the ribbon from Abra. Annie rolled the note and tied it while trying to keep the cat from untying it again. "This is my ribbon and you can't have it."

Okay, so she had no life. Outside of teaching, her daily conversations consisted of talking to a cat and painting.

While she tucked the parchment into her smock, hiding it from Abra's mischievous paws, Annie wondered yet again who "they" were—the people that Alice and Alexi were with. "They" were probably some kind of cult, which was what the police department had concluded even without the note. Annie had showed it to Awai only, for fear that the police would take it and lose it somewhere in all the shuffle of paperwork. That note was too important—it was her only link to her cousins.

Yeah, the twins were likely hidden up in the Tahoe area in some kind of back-to-nature commune. Yet, Annie couldn't believe that Alexi could possibly have been brainwashed enough to live with a cult—she was too damn pigheaded and stubborn. Alice, too, but she had a gentler side that could more easily be swayed than Alexi.

Even with the note, though, Annie had never stopped her search for her twin cousins. She had hired private investigator after private investigator, but every lead turned up empty. It was as if her cousins had vanished to another planet or something.

Using her free hand, Annie pulled her smock and T-shirt away from her breasts to allow a little cool air to flow through. It was an unusually warm day, and sweat had beaded on her skin. She had very large breasts to go along with her size 16 figure, and when she was home she preferred to go with no bra.

Even though she was inexperienced sexually, she had plenty of fantasies. It made her feel naughty and kind of sexy to be clad only in her white T-shirt and black jeans, with no underwear on at all.

Her pussy tingled and her nipples tightened as a thought crossed her mind to try taking off all her clothes and painting in the nude. Should she?

Why not? No one would see.

But what if someone stops by?

Well, she'd settle for leaving her jeans on and taking off only her shirt.

Annie whipped off her smock and pulled her T-shirt over her head, causing her braid to flip over her shoulder again. She tossed the shirt and smock onto the taupe leather couch behind her.

Closing her eyes, Annie brought her hands to her breasts, allowing her fantasies to take over. As usual, a dark, mysterious, faceless man filled her thoughts. As she imagined his hands on her nipples, she tweaked and tugged at them, feeling a response shoot down to her folds. She moved her hips in time with the movements, causing her jeans to rub against her clit as she imagined the man licking and sucking her.

Annie tilted her head back as she continued to play with her nipples. Her braid fell and swung across her skin, a teasing caress against her naked back. No one would believe her fantasies. She was the boring, staid college professor who never had time to date, and wasn't considered a worthy selection. But her fantasies . . . She had often imagined what it would feel like to have a man between her thighs, to have his cock sliding in and out of her core.

And in her most secret fantasies, she had two men pleasuring her at once . . . or even a man and a woman.

Shame on me.

Annie grinned at her own brazen thoughts. Until she was eighteen, she had been raised as a southern lady. She learned that sex was something you didn't do until you were married. And *real* ladies certainly never talked about sex. Anything other than the missionary position with a spouse was considered evil as far as her sanctimonious mother had been concerned.

But after leaving home and going to college, Annie's mind had opened up, freeing her to all the possibilities a woman could enjoy.

If only she could find the right man to enjoy them with.

The ache in her pussy was growing stronger and stronger, a tight spiral connected from her nipples to her belly to her slit. She moved her hips faster so that

17

the jeans rubbed her clit even harder until she reached that special place.

She gave a small cry as a series of mini-orgasms rippled through her, and more of her juices soaked the heavy denim of her jeans. Warmth flushed over her skin and her core pulsed as though milking a cock and drawing out her mystery man's seed.

What would a man's come smell like, taste like? Brie and salty tapioca pudding, that's what Awai said once. Just a casual comment, driving home to Annie how little first-hand information she had about intimacy. Her knowledge was confined to what she learned from literature and the imaginations of her paintbrushes . . . and the few naughty Web sites she had dared to visit.

"Brie and tapioca. Well, y'all, Annie likes both."

She lifted her eyelids and stared again at the blank canvas as she let her hands slide from her breasts and down her full waist. She felt more relaxed, her mind cleared of stress and ready to open up to her artistic imagination.

With renewed determination, Annie raised her head and pushed away thoughts of her missing cousins. Her braid fell forward over her shoulder as she attacked her canvas, losing herself in swirls of blues and grays. When she worked on a landscape, she tended to block out the rest of the world and to get lost in thoughts and feelings of the moment. She truly was in her own little world.

* * *

Persistent knocking at the front door jarred Annie from her artistic trance. She blinked the fog of colors and shapes from her mind, slowly returning to reality. A glance to the window told her that hours had fled by rather than minutes since she'd started working on her painting. The sun now hung low over the ocean, its golden ripples leading from the glowing orb across the water to the shore. A spectacular sunset of oranges, blues, and pinks streaked the horizon.

More knocks, and Annie frowned as she eyed the door. Should she answer, or hope whomever it was went away?

"Annie! I know you're in there!" Awai's no-nonsense voice sliced through the door like a diamond saw. "Stop moping and open up."

"I'm not moping," Annie grumbled under her breath. She dropped her brush into her waiting container of turpentine, climbed off the stool, and stretched her cramped muscles. The movement caused cool air to rush over her nipples, and they stood out hard and tight. Heat flushed over Annie as she realized she was still naked from the waist up. She quickly grabbed her T-shirt, and yanked it over her head.

"Annie!" Awai's tone was notched up to her *I'm-gonna-huff-and-puff-and-blow-your-house-down* voice.

"Hold on to your britches," Annie shouted. She pushed her glasses up her nose, threw her braid over her shoulder, and padded across the worn carpet to the door. Abra blinked green eyes and watched from her perch on the back of the couch. The cat had her little chin up high, doing her best to show she was queen of Annie's realm.

"What, are you naked or something?" Awai said from outside, and Annie's cheeks heated even more. "Open the damn door already."

"You have about as much patience as a hurricane." When Annie reached the door she wiped her sweating palms on her black jeans. She didn't bother to look through the peephole—no doubt at all it was Awai, the human whirlwind. She unlatched the chain lock, then opened the door.

As always, Awai was sheer elegance with her black hair in a neat chignon at her nape and wearing one of her usual designer outfits. This one had a black skirt and matching mandarin-collared jacket, her blouse a splash of amethyst in a vivid but gorgeous contrast.

Awai held two paper bags, one in each arm. "Took you long enough," she said before Annie had a chance to greet her. "Damn southerners. Everything's slow and easy."

Awai blew through the doorway and Annie was left looking out into the late-afternoon sunshine instead of at her aunt. "Uh, hello?"

The warm smell of fresh baked bread and something spicy drifted behind Awai as she headed straight into the apartment's kitchenette. Annie's stomach growled.

"I heard that," Awai said as she plopped the bags onto the counter. Without pause, she went to the oven, and turned it on. "I knew you'd be painting and moping."

"I told you already—I wasn't moping." Annie shut the front door and followed Awai into the tiny kitchen, the linoleum cool to her bare feet. "What in heaven's name are you doing?"

"Making us dinner." Awai smiled as her dark eyes met Annie's. "I figured you'd need more than just Abra for company this evening."

Annie raised an eyebrow. "You don't cook."

"Ah, but I make one hell of a mean warmed-up lasagna." Awai reached for one of the shopping bags and pulled out a loaf of French bread, a packaged salad, a bottle of Annie's favorite brand of merlot, and an aluminum pan with MAMA MIA'S ITALIAN GRILL stamped across the cardboard top.

"Mmmmm. My favorite." Annie peeked in the other bag. "Oooh, and you brought spumoni, too. I'll put it in the freezer, Auntie."

Awai gave Annie "the look" and said, "I've told you not to call me that. I'm only a couple of years older than you."

With a grin, Annie replied, "Oh, but it's so much fun to get you good and riled."

Awai sniffed and turned back to the lasagna.

Annie had to admit it was fun chatting with Awai, and it helped not to be alone while she was thinking about her missing cousins. Awai was actually their aunt by marriage, not blood, and she only had four years on Annie, who had just passed her thirtieth birthday.

Awai's being there to help her through this tough

day reminded Annie of that night a year ago when she'd taken Alexi out for drinks and dinner to help get her mind off of Alice.

The night she up and disappeared. Some idea that was, getting her drunk.

With everything being pre-prepared, it wasn't long before dinner was served. Annie and Awai sat at the small oak table in the kitchen nook and Abra rubbed her head against Annie's feet beneath the table. Awai chatted about the latest account she'd won over to her advertising firm, and of the gorgeous blond man she'd just met at the club last night.

"Which club?" Annie asked before taking a sip of her merlot.

As her eyes met Annie's, Awai gave a small shrug. "A BDSM club."

Annie choked on her wine and it shot up her nose. She grabbed her napkin and managed to cover her mouth before she spewed merlot everywhere.

"Are you all right, sweets?" Awai asked as if she'd just said she'd found toilet paper on sale at the grocery store instead of announcing she'd gone to a BDSM club.

When Annie had sufficiently recovered, she patted her mouth with the napkin then set it on her empty plate. "That's why you were wearing that tight leather dress and those thigh-high boots when I came by to ask you to go with me to Alexi's last year. You weren't off to a masquerade party. You were going to a BDSM club."

Awai smiled and raised her glass. "Does it bother you that I'm a Dominatrix? That's Domme for short."

Annie almost choked again as she visualized Awai wearing that black leather number and whipping a submissive male. "Um, no. Not at all."

Cocking her head to one side, Awai said, "You should come with me sometime and find a good Dom. You're a born submissive, you know."

"I don't think so." Annie shook her head. "I'm not into, ah, whips and handcuffs."

"It's not all about whips, chains, and pain, Annie." Awai pushed her plate aside and folded her arms on the table as she gave Annie that penetrating look of hers that was sure to have won over plenty of accounts . . . and probably submissives, too. "For a sub, giving up control is more than bondage, more than pleasure and pain. It's power. You have total control over your Master's pleasure. You hold all the cards."

Meeting Awai's gaze head-on, Annie asked, "Why are you a Domme?"

With a shrug, Awai leaned back in her chair. "I enjoy having men obeying my every whim."

"Like they do at the agency?" Annie asked as she arched one eyebrow.

Awai's mouth curved into a half smile. "Something like that."

Annie pulled her braid over her shoulder and absently played with the end of it. "If the submissive has all the control, then why aren't you a sub?"

For a moment Awai was silent. When she finally spoke she said, "Until I truly learned the concept behind BDSM, I always thought the Domme had the power." She brushed imaginary lint off her black skirt. "By the time I figured out otherwise, I had learned all about being a Domme—and now, I enjoy it too much to switch." But something in Awai's eyes held just a tinge of regret.

Before Annie could respond, Awai said, "How about I come over in the morning, and we'll head over to Macy's? They have a big sale going on, and I could use a new suit."

No doubt Awai had changed the subject because the reason she'd become a Domme was something she didn't want to talk about. Perhaps she even regretted being a Domme instead of a submissive. It would take a hell of a man to dominate Awai, though. Annie didn't think men like that existed on Earth.

Even though Awai lived in San Francisco, closer than Annie, she always insisted on picking Annie up to go to the city. Awai had a Mercedes SL600, a sleek sports car, and she loved to drive it every chance she got.

"I could use a few things, too." Annie smiled and gave a slow nod. "Why don't you drop by around ten?"

"Ten sharp." Awai pushed her chair back, gracefully stood, and headed toward the easel in the living room. "So, what are you working on? Something depressing, right?"

Annie rolled her eyes, but then she realized she had no idea what she'd done during those hours of painting today. With Abra at her heels, Annie followed Awai to the easel.

Awai pushed the stool out of the way, then folded

her arms and pursed her lips as she studied the painting. "Oh, definitely morbid, but I like it."

Annie's frown deepened, but when she reached the easel and stopped in front of the canvas, her jaw dropped.

Cocking one eyebrow, Awai cut Annie a questioning glance. "Looks like it came right out of *Wuthering Heights*."

"Yeah, it does." Annie's practiced eye scanned her work. It wasn't quite finished, but it was damn good if not murky and mysterious. Maybe it was a sign that she was more down about her cousins' disappearances than she'd thought.

A sprawling but gloomy mansion stood dark and foreboding in the background with only a single window dimly lit from within, as if by candlelight. Lightning illuminated the scene just enough that the viewer could see skeleton trees bowing close to the ground from raging winds, and in the distance whitecaps dotted a body of water below sheer black cliffs. In the lower right-hand corner was a single magnolia bloom lying on the ground, its petals pure cream beside a shadow.

She narrowed her gaze. A man's shadow. How odd.

"Well, this is interesting," Awai said, breaking into Annie's thoughts. "How did you come up with it?"

Annie shook her head. "I have no idea. The twins still missing . . . maybe it's bothering me even more than I thought."

Unable to bear the sheer strangeness of seeing a painting she had obviously created without remembering a damned thing about it, Annie turned away from the canvas. She forced a smile for Awai's benefit and tried to ignore a creeping sense that the painting was somehow . . . staring at her.

"Well, come on," Awai said. "Chop, chop. We've got spumoni waiting."

Relieved, Annie followed Awai away from the mystery on the canvas. She'd deal with it later—probably with scissors.

Awai stayed for a while longer, long enough to share the spumoni and to polish off the bottle of wine. Annie wasn't much of a drinker usually, and tonight she'd had two glasses of merlot. She felt mellow and relaxed, and definitely ready for bed.

Once Awai had left for her San Francisco apartment, Annie tried to make herself stay away from the painting. She had decided to deal with it in the morning. In the sunshine. And yet, it pulled at her.

Mumbling a few wine-enhanced curses, she finally gave up and moved the easel in front of her overstuffed armchair. Still feeling the merlot, she sat and studied her day's work, her elbow resting on her knee, her chin in her hand. Her braid fell over her opposite shoulder as she tried to interpret her own work. Abra bounded onto the armrest and started batting the end of Annie's braid.

Where the heck did I get this from?

The picture had a brooding, Gothic feel to it. It was unlike her usual landscapes and seascapes, but was still in her distinctive style. The painting was fascinating, really. She rarely had dwellings in her work, and this mausoleum of a mansion was beyond anything she thought herself capable of. Perhaps it was so captivating because it reminded her of the Gothic romance novels her grandmother was always reading when she was young and still lived in Tennessee.

At least it's not giving me the creeps anymore. Who cares where it came from? It's good. That's what matters. For a moment, she smiled, studying the mysterious lines and shadows.

"Maybe I have a dark, wild side after all. Yeah, right." Stifling a yawn, Annie rose and turned away from the painting when she heard the crack of thunder. Abra hissed and arched her back, then darted under the end table. Lights in the apartment flickered.

Everything went completely dark.

Annie frowned. They never had thunderstorms in the Bay Area because of the cool onshore flow of air from the Pacific. She started to go to the window when a flash lit up her dark apartment for a moment. Thunder boomed again, rattling her windows.

But the lightning flash hadn't come from outside.

It had come from her painting.

A strange buzzing started in Annie's ears as she moved back toward the painting—and her heart started pounding like mad.

She saw the same scene she had painted, only now it looked like a very tall and narrow television screen rather than a canvas. It was raining in the picture and trees swayed in fierce gusts of wind. She could even hear the haunting sound of whistling wind and could feel wet air blowing from the painting. It rushed across her face and misted her glasses. Something that looked like a very large cat stalked across the picture . . . a white tiger with black stripes.

Abra hissed again from beneath the end table, this time louder and much more fierce.

Goose bumps prickled Annie's skin and her nipples pebbled beneath her white T-shirt.

"Too much wine, sugar," she murmured as she pulled off her glasses that were now too fogged to see through. "This is why you don't normally drink."

Although hallucinating after only two goblets of wine was mighty strange.

Lightning flashed in the picture again and Annie jumped. In the brief illumination, she saw the magnolia bloom—only this time a man was holding it.

A man. In the picture. Looking directly at her.

He moved closer so that he filled the scene and she could hardly see anything around him. Wind tugged at his black hair and clothing, which were soaked from the rain. He was dressed in an equally black shirt and pants, but he was too close for her to be able to see what he wore on his feet. His eyes were black, too. Dark and haunting.

The man held his free hand out to her, and she took an automatic step back.

"Come, Annie," he said in a deep, husky voice that caused a thrill to zip from her belly to her pussy. "It is time."

CHAPTER TWO

A PECULIAR SENSATION SWEPT OVER ANNIE. IT was the most surreal moment of her life and she couldn't help but wonder if perhaps she was dreaming. No way had her painting come alive, and no way was a man holding out his hand to her and telling her to come with him.

Thunder boomed and Abra gave a loud *"Yerowl"* from her hiding place.

"Come, Annie." The sexy timbre of his voice and the sound of his unusual accent caused a sensual shiver to trail down her spine. "The path will soon close."

Path. The path will soon close.

"Alice and Alexi." Annie clenched her hand around her glasses as she spoke to the man in the picture. "You know them?"

He gave a slow nod. "They are in Tarok."

Annie took a deep breath. This was bizarre enough that it could really be happening.

That or she'd passed out on her living room floor and was dreaming it all.

"*Now,* Annie." His voice had a harder edge to it, a dominating command that brought her to attention immediately.

His voice was so compelling that she found herself stepping forward. She put her hand up to the painting to touch it, and her hand went into it. Not through the canvas, but *into* the scene. She immediately felt rain upon her wrist and the back of her hand. Cold air blasted against her skin, air that smelled of salt and brine from the ocean, mingling with the rain.

She started to withdraw when the man reached out of the painting and grabbed her by the shoulders.

Annie cried out in shock and surprise and instinctively tried to wrench herself free. But the man was far too strong. He pulled her forward, into the painting, dragging her into the canvas's frame.

A strange sensation whooshed over her, as if she were being pulled through a giant bowl of cake batter. For a moment, everything went dark and she felt like she was floundering in a black hole filled with that same gooey batter.

In the next instant, her feet touched wet ground, mud and grass squishing between her bare toes. She found herself held tight in the man's steel embrace, her arms trapped between his body and hers. He was huge, a good eight inches taller than her five foot nine, and his muscular frame made her size 16 body suddenly feel little.

She'd never felt petite in all her life until now. It was strangely exciting and frightening all at once to find herself small and helpless in a man's arms.

Rain pummeled their bodies but Annie barely noticed as the man's intense black gaze captured hers. A flare of recognition and desire sparked in his eyes, and then it was gone as if buried deep within the black depths.

"Do I need to guard my bollocks with you?" He studied her features as he spoke then answered his own question. "I think not. You are unlike Darronn's Alexi, the tigress. You seem more like . . . a kitten."

"My claws can be sharp," Annie responded, her southern accent growing stronger as she tried to withdraw from his grasp, but it was hopeless. She might as well have been struggling to climb out of a straightjacket. "Where are Alexi and Alice? What have y'all done with my cousins?"

Lightning illuminated the landscape followed by the bellow of thunder. Hair rose on the back of Annie's neck. The smell of ozone mingled with fresh rain and the dank smell of the moors.

The man scooped Annie up and into his arms so fast that her world spun and she gasped in surprise. Automatically, she grabbed onto his neck to keep him from dropping her.

"Wait!" She cast a glance over his shoulder as he strode toward the mansion. Like a window to her living room, she saw a rectangle cut into the sky. Through it she saw her overstuffed chair, one of her paintings on the wall, and her cat clock. Abra jumped onto the armchair, put one paw up to the rectangle, gave a loud *"Yerowl!"* and bared her teeth.

Panic gripped Annie. She couldn't leave Abra, and she couldn't leave without writing a note to Awai.

She clenched her glasses tighter in her hand as she looked up at the dark, powerful man carrying her. "I need to get Abra, my cat—" Another lightning bolt struck and the crash of thunder was even closer, cutting off her words. The man's strides grew even wider, bringing them closer to the mansion. "And I have to leave a note for my aunt," she said, talking now over the keening winds. "Awai will freak if I disappear, too."

"It is too late," he said as he jogged up massive stone steps to the mansion. "You will not be able to return until a new path opens."

She looked back and her heart sank to her bare muddy toes.

The window to her living room was gone.

Her heart pounded. What would happen to Abra? Then she remembered that Awai was coming over in the morning. She had a key to the apartment and she would make sure Abra was taken care of.

Karn shoved aside the possessive feelings the maiden inspired in him as he opened the manse doors with his magic. After he strode into the foyer, he used his powers to shut the doors, slamming them closed and causing the sound to reverberate through his mansion.

Carefully, he set his nearly drowned kitten onto her muddy feet on the flagstone floor and grasped her by her upper arms to hold her steady. Raindrops rolled from her wet hair, over her cheeks, and from the tip of her nose. Wide, warm brown eyes stared up at him, expressive eyes filled with a mixture of fear, confusion, and desire. Her lips parted as if she asked for his kiss.

Moors and skies but he wanted this woman.

His grip on her tightened as he studied her in a slow and deliberate perusal starting with her face and then resting on her chest. His cock grew tighter against his breeches as he saw that her white tunic was drenched. The dark circles of her nipples were clearly outlined against the wet fabric.

Waiting for his lips, his mouth, his teeth.

When his eyes met Annie's, she was biting her lower lip and her cheeks were red.

"You are a beauty," he murmured without intending to.

Her cheeks flamed brighter yet. "I . . . ah . . . I need to know what's going on."

"You are mine. That is all you need to know." He drew her flush against him and captured her mouth with his.

Annie gasped against his lips, allowing him to dart his tongue inside. He took possession of her, claiming what rightfully belonged to him and *only him*. A moan escaped his kitten and then he swore she purred into his mouth. Her tongue flicked tentatively against his, as if uncertain, perhaps timid.

Could his mate be inexperienced in the ways of men?

The mere thought was both heady and intoxicating, and nearly caused him to roar.

All thought had fled Annie's mind. There was no longer past or future, just now. Her head spun and her body tingled from head to nipples to toes. She'd only experienced a few clumsy kisses before, and nothing had prepared her for this. Was the room supposed to whirl and was she supposed to feel like her knees were going to give out, as if she was drunk?

His tongue tangled with hers and she followed his lead. It felt incredible to have him inside her, and even though she didn't know him, she *wanted* him.

Oh, my heavens, did she want him.

A rumble rose up in the man's chest and she would have sworn it was the purr of a tiger or lion. Her pussy and nipples ached and her entire body was on fire.

When he broke the kiss and pulled just inches away, he stared at her with an expression of surprise, maybe even amazement. Had he felt what she had? A crazy insane lust that made her want to slide between the sheets with this man.

Better yet, she'd like to go at it right here, right now.

"I don't even know your name," she whispered.

"Karn." It came out almost harsh, and his eyes were once again barren of emotion.

Annie tried to pull away but he still held tight. So tight that her arms had gone numb. "You're hurting me, Karn," she managed to say. "Think you could let up a bit?"

"My apologies, kitten." He released her and let his hands fall to his sides. "Welcome to Diamond Hall, your new home."

Annie frowned at his statement, but she couldn't help glancing around her as he gestured to their surroundings. She'd been so mesmerized by Karn that she hadn't taken the time to notice where they were. The mansion was stately and elegant, but dark and depressing as hell. She was in a mammoth-sized entryway looking into an enormous room. Stairs made of carved dark wood like mahogany curved at either side, rising up to the floor above. Around her was elegant furniture in the same dark wood, and everything cushioned in sapphire blue. Heavy blue velvet drapes shrouded every window. Between the stairs was a set of closed double doors, and to either side of her were more doors, all closed tight.

It smelled of burning candles, sandalwood, and a hint of roses. Outside, the storm roared on but it was muffled now.

Annie folded her arms across her breasts as her gaze returned to meet Karn's. She tried to keep her teeth from chattering, but she was cold, wet, muddy, confused, and heaven help her, but this dark and mysterious man turned her on.

"Forgetting your manners, your Highness?" someone said in a small, high-pitched voice, causing Annie to jerk her attention toward a tiny woman. Annie blinked—she could almost swear she saw sparkles all around her. As if floating on air, the three-foot-tall woman approached them. Her green skirt reached the floor, long enough to cover her feet and trail over the mottled gray flagstones.

Where had she come from? All the doors were still closed.

The elderly woman wiped her hands on a flour-coated blue apron. Her cheeks were full and pale, her eyes like bright-blue buttons against the whiteness of her skin. She was short and squat and Annie was reminded of one of those toys she'd played with as a child. The ones that wobbled but never fell down.

"For shame, your Highness." The woman gave a sniff in Karn's direction when she reached them, then turned her attention toward Annie. "A drowned cat you be, Mistress. A king should know better. Come with Beya and I will see to your bath."

Annie's jaw dropped. *Karn is a king?*

"*I* will escort Annie to her chambers, Beya." Karn's baritone caused Annie's pulse to race. "Please see to it the servants draw her bath and leave."

Beya sniffed again. "At once, Sire." She gave a curt bow and turned, her skirt swirling over the floor. And then she vanished—only a few sparkles remained where she had been only moments before.

Annie gasped and shot her gaze back to Karn's. "Where'd she go?"

He raised an eyebrow. "To see to my instructions."

Annie flipped her braid over her shoulder and frowned. "That isn't what I meant."

Karn took a step toward the staircase. "Follow me."

"I'm not following you anywhere." Annie put her hands on her full hips and glared at him. "I want to see my cousins and I'd like to see them *now*."

His jaw tightened and his nostrils flared as he came

back to stand mere inches from her. "You will see them when I believe you are ready."

Ooooh! Now he had her good and riled.

"I don't know who the hell you think you are, mister, but I've had enough." Her southern accent grew stronger and she was talking fast like she always did when she was angry. "I want to see Alice and Alexi right this minute."

Karn scowled so fiercely that she almost stepped back. He gave a growl and grasped her around the waist. Her world spun and she shrieked as he flung her over his shoulder and marched toward the stairs.

Heat flushed throughout Annie, but she was too stunned to know what to do next. Her wet T-shirt fell up to her neck and her bare breasts were rubbing against his leather shirt, and her braid flopped over her head. She was still gripping her glasses with one hand and was trying to pull her shirt back to her waist without a lot of luck.

While he climbed the stairs her thoughts raced, imagining every horror her mind could come up with. What if he was some madman and he was going to lock her away? Worse yet, what if he intended to kill her? What if he had hurt Alice and Alexi, or maybe killed them?

But her gut told her this powerful man wasn't that kind of dangerous. He was some kind of dangerous, but not *that* kind.

More like he was perilous to her libido . . . although she couldn't find anything wrong with the thought of enjoying this man in bed. Just the mere image of that made her pussy ache in a way she'd never experienced before.

After he reached the top of the stairs, Karn headed down a dark hall lit by sconces fastened along the walls. The walls were paneled in the same dark mahogany the downstairs furniture was made from.

All the blood had rushed to Annie's head but she still had the presence of mind to admire the flex of his muscular ass beneath his leather breeches while the earthy, virile scent of him surrounded her.

He carried her through a door and into a beautiful room. Draped over his shoulder the way she was, she only caught a glimpse of it but it seemed much more feminine than the rest of the house with rose velvet cushions, lots of flowers, a full-length mirror, and a hearth with a fire crackling. The fire, along with the soft glow of candlelight, gave the room warmth, yet it was still somehow dark and oppressive, as though it needed something or someone to give it life.

Karn strode through another set of doors then slid her from his shoulder and set her on her feet on the surprisingly warm flagstone floor. For a moment Annie clung to him while she regained her balance, and studied her surroundings.

He had carried her into a bathroom of sorts. The huge room was made of dark stone, the centerpiece being a pool built into a corner.

A small waterfall tumbled from a corner and greenery filled the room. Palms, vines, and other exotic plants obscured the ceiling and a good portion of the walls, making it feel more like a jungle hideaway than a bathroom. Steam rose from the pool's surface, bringing the perfume of orchids to her nose. The water looked incredibly warm and inviting, especially since she was freezing cold, not to mention mussed and muddy.

How had they drawn the bath so quickly?

Magic.

Nah. Couldn't be.

"Remove your clothes," Karn said, and her attention immediately snapped to him.

Annie stepped back, her cheeks burning. "Beg your pardon?"

The man advanced on her. "If you do not, I will remove them for you."

Her jaw dropped and she knew she had to be ten shades of red. "You wouldn't."

Karn cocked a brow. "Indeed."

He would.

Crap.

Annie's whole body caught fire with embarrassment. "Well, turn your back then."

His brow raised a notch higher.

"Please?" The word came out in a tortured whisper because for the first time in her adult life she was about to undress in front of a man, and it scared the hell out of her.

Karn studied her for a moment, then folded his arms across his chest and turned his back to her.

Annie never undressed so fast in her life. She was

worried he'd turn back around and see her before she got into the water, and she wasn't taking any chances. Not only was this the first time she was taking her clothing off around a man, she was self-conscious about her full figure. She set her glasses down on a rock shelf, flung off her T-shirt, shimmied out of her jeans, and practically bolted into the pool.

When Annie was sitting on a rock bench, slumped so that she was up to her neck in the warm water, she held her knees tightly together, folded her arms across her chest, then said, "Okay, I'm in. Will you go now so that I can take my bath in peace?"

Karn turned back to her and studied her long enough that she began to tremble beneath his gaze.

Then, with a wave of his hand, his clothing vanished.

As in disappeared like magic.

As in he was standing completely naked before her.

Annie's jaw hit the water. Oh, heavens above but the man was gorgeous from his ebony eyes to his dark-brown hair, powerful arms . . . narrow hips . . . even the scars across his muscled chest made him even more exciting, possibly dangerous.

And oh, my God . . . Karn's cock was so thick and so big she was sure it would be considered a lethal weapon in all fifty states.

And then Karn was walking across the room, straight toward the sunken pool, straight toward her.

CHAPTER THREE

THE MIXTURE OF EMOTION IN ANNIE'S EXPRES-
sion told Karn how innocent his kitten truly
was. His senses told him without a doubt that
she had never been with a man before. Amazement,
surprise, terror, and definitely desire flashed in her expressive eyes as she stared at his erection. He had sensed
that desire the moment he had allowed her to see him
through the path opening, and had felt her need in her
kiss.

Well and good. If I must have a bride, better that she enjoy me.

The candle flame flickered, casting warm light over
the pool and his mate. He scented the air and with his
keen senses caught the essence of her arousal blending
with the vanilla musk of her skin and the orchid perfume his servants had put in the bath water.

Yes, his beautiful kitten's desire matched his equally.

Brown eyes wide, Annie pressed back against the

bathing pool's rock wall, her arms folded across her luscious breasts. "W-what are you doing?"

Instead of answering, he stepped into the pool's warm waters. It skimmed his bollocks as he walked toward Annie, his eyes never moving from hers.

Her cheeks went crimson and she bit her lip and looked away from him. "I-I don't bathe with men I don't know."

Karn eased onto the underwater seat beside Annie so that his hip was firmly against hers, his bicep against her shoulder. She was trembling and all the bare flesh he could see had flushed a lovely shade of rose.

The lust raging through him came as a great surprise. This was supposed to be a duty. He hadn't expected it to be a pleasure—or to find himself so close to being out of control. He wished to slide between her fair thighs and take what was rightfully his.

But he would not take her until she was ready for him.

He gently stroked the generous curve of her waist, reveling in her well-rounded figure. The fact that she wasn't skin and bones pleased him greatly. This was a woman meant to be made love to.

To fuck, he reminded himself firmly. *Not love. Fucking.*

"There will be no secrets between us," he said as he caressed her thigh, almost to her mound, then trailed his finger up her belly, between her breasts, and to her jawline. "Whether it is your mind, your body, your heart, your soul, you will share openly with me," he said as he captured her chin.

Annie's heart beat so fast and so hard she was sure anyone in the mansion could hear it. The feel of his naked skin brushing against hers along with his calloused fingertips on her thigh were causing a five-alarm blaze to heat up all her senses.

How did she end up unclothed in a tub with the most gorgeous man she'd ever met?

"I don't understand what's going on." She hugged herself tighter as he held her chin and her gaze captive. "I came with you to find my cousins, not to get it on with you."

He moved his hand to her face to gently trace her lower lip with his thumb. The sensual touch, the look in his eyes, made Annie positively melt. Good heavens but she wanted him. She wanted to reach out and to run her hands all over his powerful biceps, along the scars on his massive chest, his washboard stomach, and muscled thighs. And his cock . . . she wanted to touch him from balls to tip . . . and taste him.

She'd gone from inexperienced virgin to wanton woman in ten seconds flat.

"You are where you belong, kitten," Karn murmured as he continued to stroke her bottom lip. "Soon enough you will be with your family. First, you must be well versed in the ways of pleasuring your king."

"You're not my king." Annie frowned, which wasn't easy to do when she was so turned on and he was touching her lip like that. "You're not talking sense."

Karn put one arm behind her, like a guy making his moves by putting his arm on a seat back before closing in on his date. He moved closer so that his body was firmly against hers and Annie couldn't think anymore.

Her brain had left the building.

"I am your king, and you are my destined mate." Slowly, Karn eased his finger from her lips and down along the slender column of her neck to her collarbone that was just above water level because of the way she was slumped down. "And as such you will be trained in all the skills necessary to obey my commands and to give me pleasure."

Annie barely heard him as he spoke, and nothing he said really clicked in her brain or made sense. What happened to Annie Travis, the college professor who was a force to be reckoned with, who intimidated most men simply by her intelligence?

Her smarts had taken a hike. At this moment, she felt about as bright as a turnip.

Karn's fingers skated lower, into the water, until he reached the swell of her breast. Annie couldn't stop trembling. She didn't know what to do, what to say, how to act. This was outside her realm, something she wasn't equipped to deal with.

"Where are my cousins?" she whispered, desperately trying to say anything that would detract from the sensation of him gently skimming his fingertips along the top of her breasts, from one to the other.

"Alice and Alexi are safe and well." Karn took one of her hands and firmly tugged at it, forcing it away from her breasts. "When your training is complete, I will take you to them."

It was like he had magic in his touch, the way he pulled first one hand away from her breast, then the other, and somehow she had no inclination to cover them again. Instead, she reveled in the way he gazed at her and the flare of desire in his midnight-dark eyes.

"What?" The word slipped through her lips in a low and husky tone that reflected her own need. Her brain had gone from brilliant to bimbette and she couldn't think beyond her desire for Karn.

"Mmmmm." The sound rolled from him like a deep and vibrant purr. He brought his hand to one of her breasts and held it, as though testing its weight. "Such beauty . . . waiting for my touch, and my touch alone."

As if I've been waiting all my life for you. The thought felt right to Annie, as if she *had* been waiting for him, forever.

When he withdrew his hand she almost whimpered, but then he caught one of her hands and brought it toward him. Before she fully realized what he was doing, he settled her hand right on his erection.

Annie's eyes widened and her skin flushed with heat. Automatically, she tried to snatch her hand back but he held firm.

"Do not fight me. That is your first lesson. I will ask no more—or less—of you than you want to give."

She was so confused by what was happening that she couldn't think of a suitable response.

"Feel what you do to me, kitten." He forced her fingers to close around his length, his gaze never leaving hers. "Feel how badly my cock wants to be inside you."

At his last comment, Annie's cheeks blazed. She

tore her gaze from his and looked into the water where she could clearly see his hand holding hers firmly around his erection. His cock was so big that the head actually protruded from the pool by a good five inches, and at the tiny hole at the top, a bead of fluid glistened in the candlelight.

Karn leaned down so that his lips were close to her ear, causing her to shiver. "Stroke my cock, Annie."

Using his firm grip, he forced her hand to slide down his length and back to the head. Her natural curiosity kicked in, and she focused on the feel of him against her palm as he moved her hand up and down his shaft. It felt hard, yet soft, like silk covering a steel rod. His cock was so long she wondered how it could possibly fit inside her.

"It will fit, kitten."

Annie jerked her head up and tried to stop stroking his cock, but he forced her to keep going. "You read my mind?"

"I read your eyes." A hint of a smile teased the corner of his mouth. "You have a very expressive face."

"Oh." Annie couldn't take looking into his dark gaze, she was just too embarrassed. She turned her attention back to his cock and realized that he had released her, yet she continued to stroke it on her own.

She stopped, but then Karn had his hand on the back of her head, clenching her braid, and lightly forcing her downward. "Taste me," he murmured. "I can see it in your eyes, how badly you wish to lick my cock."

A part of her said to tell this arrogant bastard to go

to hell. After all, she'd barely met the man. She could almost feel the fires of hell blazing right under her tender feet, though she'd never really given her mother's rantings much due.

But another part of her wanted this . . . *education.* Yes. Like she'd dreamed about, but had never found the right man to teach her.

She relaxed, giving in to his prompts, allowing him to lower her head. When her lips met the head of his cock a thrill shot from her mouth to her nipples to her pussy. It felt so soft against her lips and so hard in her hand. The thrill was even more intense knowing that she was the cause of his arousal.

A smile touched her lips as she flicked her tongue over the tiny hole at the head of his cock and tasted the fluid beaded there. It was salty and sweet, and she liked it. She wanted more of it.

Karn was moving her other hand up and down the five inches of his shaft that was underwater. The man's cock was a good ten inches total, but she was able to take him deep enough that her lips met the pool before she moved her mouth back up his shaft again.

When Karn groaned, Annie swore she had never felt such a thrill in her life. *She* was in control of this man's pleasure.

And then it hit her . . . what Awai had said only hours ago at Annie's dinner table, *"For a sub, giving up control is more than bondage, more than pleasure and pain. It's power. You have total control over your Master's pleasure. You hold all the cards."*

She held all the cards.

The thought fueled Annie's excitement. She thought about everything she'd ever read about sex, about what men enjoyed, and she did her best to translate printed words to real actions.

The books definitely didn't do this experience justice!

She used her tongue along his length and applied gentle suction as her hand continued to work his shaft and she thought about what Awai had said. No doubt this man was a Dominant, and it all made sense when she recalled what he'd said about training her to pleasure him.

He wanted her as his submissive.

But was that what she wanted?

Her body burned with heat, her senses filled with Karn's musk and the tropical scents of the trees and bushes surrounding the pool. Warm water lapped at her body and teased her breasts as she moved up and down his shaft.

"Stroke my bollocks," Karn commanded in a voice that was gravelly with lust.

Annie found herself instinctively following his command while she continued to give him fellatio. She brought her hand through the water, up to his balls and felt their weight in her hand. She gently squeezed.

Karn literally growled.

His balls drew up, his cock went rigid, and come filled her mouth.

It tasted different, like nothing she'd ever tasted before. From Awai's comment, Annie had half expected it to taste like Brie or tapioca, but it was different. Sweet yet salty.

Knowing that she had brought him such pleasure and had made him come was a powerful aphrodisiac. It made her want him even more. It didn't matter that he was a stranger—she wanted to feel his hands on her body, and to feel his cock deep within her core.

She sucked him, drawing more of his fluid into her mouth and down her throat. Karn clenched his hand tighter in her hair and tugged on her braid.

"Enough!" He pulled her away from him so that she was again sitting up and looking at him. Perspiration beaded his face and his eyes had a wild look to them. "If you were not an innocent, I would fuck you now," he said, his chest rising and falling as though he'd just run a mile.

The way he said *I would fuck you now* made wild sensations tear through her body.

What's stopping you, sugar? went through her mind as though the alien bimbette was suddenly back and taking over her brain.

"I will fuck you, soon." His muscles flexed and his jaw tightened. "I will drive my cock into your quim and take what is mine."

Annie thought about telling him she wasn't his, but she couldn't. She actually liked the idea of belonging to this man. The idea of him considering her as *his*.

Abruptly, Karn stood and moved in front of her. Her

gaze traveled up the powerful thighs and the length of his cock that was as impressively erect as before, even though she'd just given him a blow job.

Oh, my god. Annie brought her wet hand to her lips where she could feel him as if she was still going down on him. *I just gave a total stranger a blow job, and a king no less.*

While she was still coming to grips with her first sexual experience, Karn grasped her upper arms and brought her to her feet. For a moment, he simply studied her eyes then brushed his lips over hers in a devastatingly sensual caress.

Annie moaned and allowed him to lead her to the falls. He held up his hand and a large gold ring lowered from the palm trees shading the pool. She was nearsighted and didn't have her glasses on to know for sure, but the ring didn't look like it was attached to anything . . . as if it was suspended in midair.

As she brought her gaze back to Karn, he held out one palm and two wide red ribbons appeared. As if out of nowhere. Annie was still staring wide-eyed while he took one of her hands and tied one of the ribbons around her wrist.

"How do you do that?" Her gaze traveled his muscular chest until she reached his face. "The ribbons. They just appeared, like magic."

"It *is* magic." He brought her wrist high over her head and pressed her back against the smooth stone of the falls. Water rushed over her body, caressing her as his eyes traveled over her breasts. "The talent to manipulate and retrieve objects is innate in my species. It is a trait nurtured in my race from the time we are mere cubs."

She was about to ask him about the cubs thing and about magic when she realized he'd tied her wrist above her head.

Panic and surprise surged through Annie as she pulled against the bond. "What are you doing?"

"Binding you," he said, even as he was raising her other wrist and tying it above her head.

"What in heaven's name . . ."Annie struggled against her bonds even though she knew it was futile. A combination of anger, fear, embarrassment, and desire surged through her. With her hands tied high above her head, her body was completely on display, as if she was an offering to a god.

And Karn was the god.

Satisfaction gleamed in her god's ebony eyes as she stopped struggling. He stepped so close she felt the brush of his cock against her belly. Her pussy flooded and her mind went straight back to bimbette mode. She couldn't think, couldn't rationalize. All she knew was that she wanted this man.

And amazingly enough, she liked how it felt to be tied up and at his mercy.

Karn pressed his body against hers, gently pushing her harder against the smooth rocks of the waterfall. The top of the falls just reached her shoulders and water continued to rush over her breasts down to her mons and along her thighs.

As he pressed his muscular form tight to her, Karn

took her braid and pulled it apart, freeing her butt-length hair and letting it fall over her breasts and back.

"Always leave your hair like this," he murmured. There was no mistaking that it was not a suggestion, but a command. "When I give you a direction, you must say, 'Yes, Sire.'"

Annie swallowed. "And what if I don't?"

Karn gave a lethal smile. "Then I must punish you."

Her eyes widened and she caught her breath as she pictured him wielding a long leather strap and taking it to her hide. "Punish . . . as in whipping me?"

He rubbed his fingers through her hair, as if he enjoyed the feel of it. "Perhaps. If that is something you would find pleasurable."

Annie couldn't think very clearly with this man's body so close to her, his musky scent filling her senses, his cock pressed to her belly, and her arms bound above her head. "I don't see how pain could be pleasurable."

"You will," he said, in a voice filled with promise.

Before she could respond, he lowered his head and flicked his tongue over one of her nipples. Annie gasped and found herself sinking into the feeling, letting her weight hang against the bindings above. Heavens, but the feeling of being bound was exciting enough. Add the sensations of warm water rushing over her, his hot mouth on her nipples, and his lower body against hers. . . . It was all so erotic and incredible that she simply gave herself up to it without question.

But when his calloused hand traveled down her

belly and cupped her mons, the butterflies in her belly went ballistic.

Heat from arousal and from embarrassment flushed over her. "I've never . . . been with a man before."

"I know, kitten," Karn murmured just as he slipped one finger into her slit. "I sensed it the moment I touched you."

Annie moaned and her knees gave out. Her wrists pulled against the restraints, but they held tight. She'd never realized how amazing it would feel to have a man touch her so intimately.

A purr rose up in him as he sucked her nipples. "So sweet, so innocent," he said, then dipped his finger into her slick core, causing her to cry out with surprise and pleasure. "And so very tight and wet."

He thrust two fingers inside her, knuckles deep, and Annie jerked against her bonds. She watched him sucking her nipples and felt his fingers moving in and out. It all seemed so surreal, yet thrilling. How could she be here now, with this gorgeous man who had claimed her as if she was his property?

But she didn't have time to think about it much longer because he was moving his lips down her belly, straight to her mons.

His tongue trailed circles in the soft hair and she heard him breathe deeply of her scent. He smiled. It embarrassed her, yet she found it exhilarating, too, that he was as turned on by her as she was turned on by him. As he bent to touch her, to smell her, she saw an unusual tattoo on his upper-right shoulder: a kind of red and gold filigree diamond. She wanted to touch it, to caress his skin, to slip her fingers into his dark hair, but the bindings held her fast.

But in the next moment she forgot all about the diamond tattoo as Karn brought his hands to her slit and opened her to his gaze.

Annie's breath caught in her chest as she watched him lave her pussy, and she cried out from the incredible feeling of his tongue licking her folds. Only in her wildest dreams had she imagined what it would feel like to have a man licking her like this. Her entire experience was certainly beyond those dreams.

Karn clenched her buttocks with one hand as he thrust two fingers into her core and pressed his face tight against her folds.

Annie's orgasm slammed into her so hard and fast that she cried out in wonder and surprise. She'd never had such an intense climax and it seemed as if it would go on forever. Her hips bucked against his face and she pulled against her restraints. But he kept on, causing one aftershock after another.

When he finally stopped, Annie was as limp as her old Raggedy Ann doll.

Karn rose up so that he was standing before her. He clenched his fist in her hair and brought his mouth to hers in a fierce kiss, and it surprised her to taste herself on his lips and tongue. When he pulled away his eyes were smoldering and she half expected him to take her virginity right then and there.

And she wanted him to. "Are you going to, ah . . ." Her face burned and she couldn't finish the question.

Apparently, he understood her only too well. "No, not yet," he said in that maddeningly low tone that gave her shivers. His grip on her hair tightened. "But do not mistake me. What you have to give is mine to take—mine and mine alone, just like you, kitten."

Annie wanted to deny the thrill his statement gave her, but she couldn't. For all of her education, books, and learning, she could find no words to deny this sexy, powerful man.

"Forever mine," he rumbled with the same word-slaying certainty that kept her from refusing him.

As Annie pulled against her bonds and felt the electric brush of his rough skin against hers, she had no idea why words were so important anyway.

CHAPTER FOUR

ANNIE BARELY HELD BACK HER TREMORS AS Karn finished soaping her body with vanilla-scented gel. The rinse was even more sensual. The way he seemed to enjoy the full curves of her body made her beyond excited for him.

By the time he freed her from her bonds, her desire for him had increased tenfold and she wanted to jump the man. The series of orgasms he'd given her merely whetted her appetite.

She was long past ready to lose her virginity.

But what about pregnancy?

"Do you have condoms?" she asked while Karn toweled her off with a thin but amazingly absorbent piece of cloth. "I don't want to get pregnant."

His eyes met hers and he gave her an amused look. "The only time men of my species can impregnate a woman is if we release our seed when we reach simultaneous climax with our mates. Our mates must also be in heat."

"Oh." Annie watched the play of his muscles and enjoyed the feel of his hands rubbing her with the cloth. "What did you mean by your species?"

He shrugged. "My people."

By his closed expression, it was obvious that he wasn't in the mood to explain further. But she still needed to find out more information about her cousins. "Where are Alice and Alexi?"

"Silence, kitten." Karn scowled and flexed his muscles. "If you wish to be punished I will gladly turn you over my knee and spank your ass."

Annie shivered. The look in his dark eyes made it clear he was serious. She swallowed back a retort and stood still as he finished drying her from her hair down to her toes. Oddly enough, the thought of being spanked by Karn excited her. Why, she couldn't say, but she had to admit that it did.

"These are your quarters," he said as he took her by her upper arm and brought her into the bedroom.

Annie pushed aside thoughts of scaling this mountain of a man. She sure as hell wasn't going to beg him for sex.

Instead, she let her gaze drift over the room and simply enjoyed the beauty of the place. Countless candles flickered throughout the bedroom from where they were arranged on top of dressers, tables, and chests. The soft lighting played over rosewood furniture and delicate flower-print cushions, giving the room a lovely, dreamy feel. If she had been asked to design the perfect room for her, this would be it.

There was even a bay window with a cushioned seat, and the drapes were pulled back so that she could see the storm was still in full force. Since the time she was a little girl, she'd always wanted a window seat to stare out at the stars.

Although tonight there were no stars visible, from what she glimpsed through the window. Outside, the storm continued to vent its wrath with keening winds, lightning flashes, and booming thunder. In the bathing room, Annie hadn't heard the tempest, but now it sounded fierce, like it might blow apart the mansion.

"Your clothing is here." Karn pointed to a rosewood trunk and the lid opened as if raised by invisible strings.

"How do you do that?" Annie asked, but snapped her mouth shut when she saw Karn's glare. Obviously, he was in no mood to chat, and she was too tired to argue or to be spanked.

When Annie went to the trunk and peeked inside, she saw stacks of clothing in beautiful hues, all so unlike the dark colors she normally wore. The bright fabrics seemed out of place from what she'd seen of the gloomy mansion, except for this one beautiful room. Of course, she hadn't seen much in the short amount of time she'd been here, but gloomy had been a dang good description for what she *had* seen.

Karn reached inside the trunk and pulled out a

sheer nightgown in sparkling gold. "Stand still," he commanded. When she obeyed, he slipped the filmy material over her head.

His jaw tightened as the glittering cloth slid over her breasts and dropped to the top of her thighs, just barely covering her mons, like a baby-doll nightie. The material clung to her curvy figure, clearly showing her pink nipples and the dark triangle between her thighs. Even though she'd just spent the last couple of hours naked with Karn, she felt exposed. Heat rose to her cheeks and she wanted to dodge under the bedcovers.

He waved his hand, and instantly he was clothed again, as quickly as he had undressed in the bathing room.

Whoa.

She bit her lip then got her courage up and asked, "Will you be sleeping in here?"

"No." The terse answer was all he gave her as he clasped her upper arm and led her to the bedside, then pulled down the covers and helped her into the bed. Like a child being tucked in at night, she found herself following his directions. The next thing she knew she was in bed with covers up to her neck.

"My chambers are on the other side of that door." He gave a nod toward a door across the room, between a potted tree with feathery blue leaves and a tall rosewood wardrobe.

The thought of only a door between them was both frightening and exhilarating all at once.

"If you have need of me, I will be in my study." Karn

gave a dismissive wave of his fingers and all candlelight snuffed out immediately, plunging the room into near darkness. Lightning flashed outside and in the brief illumination she saw his hand move again, and a small fire started crackling in the fireplace.

He leaned down, brushed his lips over her forehead then stepped back. "Sleep, kitten," he murmured before turning away and striding toward the door.

Gee, what did one say to a man who had dragged you through a picture and into another world? "Uh, good night," she finally murmured to his back, and then he was gone. The door closed behind him with a soft thump.

For a long time Annie stared up at the canopy that shrouded her bed. *What a weird day.*

No, weird didn't begin to describe it. Everything that happened was so unreal, and so surreal that she wondered if she'd wake up and find that she'd been dreaming.

Although she didn't feel like she was dreaming. Yet how could it be true? She'd been pulled through her own painting for heaven's sake. She'd given a god of a man a blow job, her first ever. And better yet, he'd tied her up with magical rings and ribbons and licked her pussy until she had the most amazing series of orgasms. Heck, she would have had sex with him, if he'd wanted to. She sure wanted him.

Her pussy ached so much that wild thoughts filled her mind. What if she slipped out of the room, found him in his study, and really did jump him? Or later, she could sneak through that door to his chambers and crawl into bed with him.

Annie rolled her eyes. With a sigh she turned onto her side and watched flames flicker and dance in the fireplace. The room was dark save for occasional lightning flashes and firelight. The flames cast haunting shadows that moved and waltzed about the bedroom like ghosts of the past.

What secrets did this mansion hold?

Just the thought of spirits made her shiver and she slid deeper under her covers. When she was a little girl she'd been afraid of the dark, and a little of that fear had always remained with her.

She missed Abra so much. Her cat had been her only companion for the last five years, and Annie was used to the calico curling up close to her neck when she slept.

Thank goodness Awai would be taking care of the poor kitty, so maybe Abra soon wouldn't feel as alone as Annie suddenly did.

At the thought of Awai, Annie frowned in the darkness. She hated the fact that now Awai would be worried sick about all three of them—Annie as well as Alexi and Alice. And Awai would be alone.

But a part of Annie was excited that she would see her missing cousins soon. For some crazy reason she trusted Karn and hoped he'd been telling her the truth that the twins were doing well and were happy.

Holding that thought tight in her heart, Annie drifted asleep.

* * *

Although in his human form, Karn paced his study like the tiger he was, his boots thunking with every step. He was surely wearing a groove through the finely woven rug arranged before his hearth. The room smelled of burning *ch'tok* wood, old books, and cedar. The fire blazing in the hearth had chased the storm-chilled air from the room, but did nothing for the chill in his heart.

Yet, mere hours in Annie's presence had threatened to warm him.

No, damn the skies. I won't allow it.

For the first time since he had gone from youth to man, he had climaxed from one woman's soft touch. He usually required two or three wenches at a time to assuage his needs.

Karn growled and clenched his fists, and tried to turn his thoughts away from Annie.

His study was filled with books and scrolls along with remembrances from the past, such as the magical wooden bird he treasured as a cub, a present from his father. And next to it was the worn war-ball he and his brothers had oft played with when they were young.

Their artistic mother had gifted all her sons with portraits of each member of the family. Karn kept them all on his study walls, even the one of his sister . . . one of the women who had taught him the uselessness of love and trust. Their mother had completed portraits of family members for each of the sons before she took ill. She never had a chance to start on a set for her youngest child and only daughter, Mikaela.

Karn scowled at the portrait of his traitorous sister. In the picture she looked so angelic, her face sweet and loving and so unlike what she had turned into.

It was just as well Mikaela had no pictures of the family. He oft considered taking down his sister's portrait, smashing it to bits, flinging it into the fireplace and burning it to cinders. But perversely he kept her picture on his study wall, another reminder to himself to keep thick boundaries around his heart and to refuse to allow anyone to penetrate its barriers.

While he paced the length of his study, Karn's thoughts continually returned to Annie. He kept seeing her brown-sugar eyes, her nut-brown hair, and her gentle smile. And her face . . . how beautiful she was when she reached climax.

She's just another woman who could betray you, Karn reminded himself. Yet instinctively he knew she was different.

Still, it frustrated him to no end that he couldn't get the sweet wench off his mind. His cock yet ached and it had taken all his restraint not to throw his future queen on the bed and fuck her many times over. Hell, he had almost taken her while she was bound in the bathing pool. He had no doubt that she wanted him, too, and he would have ensured she enjoyed the encounter.

But Annie deserved gentleness when they mated.

The first time.

It pleased him greatly that he would be the only

man to thrust his cock into her core, to take her innocence and bring her fully into her womanhood. As beautiful as Annie was, it had surprised Karn to discover his
future queen was a virgin. But there was no doubt in his
mind she was unaccustomed to a man's touch.

What was it about the maid that stirred his protec-
tive instincts? That made him crazy with need for her?

Lust, you fool, Karn all but growled to himself. That
was all he would allow his mind and soul to feel for her.
And of course he would protect what was his. After all,
he was a weretiger, and all weretigers guarded their own
with incredible fierceness.

But love . . . no.

Karn's scowl deepened. He would not allow Annie to
take residence in his heart. He would care for her, protect her, and mate with her, but he would not fall in love
with her. Too many times his heart had been ripped to
shreds, and there was no love left for him to give, save for
a very few—his brothers, nieces, and nephews. Even with
those members of his family he restrained his emotions.
He would not allow himself to care so deeply again.

An odd sound met Karn's keen hearing, even through
the storm. He paused his endless pacing. It was a tiny
noise, much like the mewling of Darronn's and Alexi's
newborn cubs.

Yet there were no cubs in Diamond Hall.

Karn instantly shifted into a tiger, fur covering his
flesh, limbs transforming into powerful legs, and sharp
teeth bared to protect his kingdom. He bounded from
the room and into the candlelit hallways toward the

manse's immense front doors where the mewling sound was loudest. When he reached the doors, he used his magic to open one and crouched, ready to pounce, should he need to.

A tiny creature sat huddled on the doorstep, drenched and shivering. The moment it saw Karn the tiger, the creature hissed, arched its back, and held up one paw with its claws bared.

Karn would have laughed had he been in his man's form. He recognized the tiny beast that had peered through the path entrance. Annie had called it Abra, and had said it was her cat. Obviously, the cat followed her through the path before it was sealed. Karn's mate had seemed concerned for the creature, and he was confident it would please her to have her companion.

If Annie was forced to be in a loveless joining, then better for her to have something with her to offer comfort.

Not giving the creature a chance to run, Karn pounced and gently caught Abra by the scruff of her neck with his teeth, careful not to hurt her.

The cat gave a fierce *"Yerowl,"* and tried to bat at Karn with her sharp little claws, but she was helpless in his grip. He turned toward the stairs after using his magic to close the door behind him.

Karn bounded up the staircase to Annie's chambers. After he quietly let himself into her room and closed the doors behind him, he took the tiny beast to the rug in front of the fireplace.

With a quick movement, Karn pinned the cat so that

she couldn't move. He proceeded to lick Abra's wet fur like he would one of his own cubs, even though he never intended to bring any into this harsh world.

Gradually, Abra relaxed as he licked her fur, and soon she began to purr as she warmed from Karn's cleaning and from the crackling fire.

While he attended to Abra, Karn was intensely aware of the sleeping woman mere feet from him. Her breathing was soft and on occasion she murmured in her sleep. His desire for her had never waned and he wanted nothing more than to shift into his man form and slide into bed with her.

What is she dreaming? he wondered. Was it about him? Or perhaps her family, of Alexi and Alice.

Why do I care?

When Abra was clean and dry, the cat drifted off to sleep. She was obviously worn out from her journey from the path to the mansion, and likely she had spent time trying to find a way in before she positioned herself at the front door and cried out for Annie to come to her.

Karn thought about carrying Abra to Annie's bed, but he didn't want to wake the sleeping creature or his sleeping mate. He stretched out beside Abra, keeping the little beast close to his chest and sharing his warmth.

As he grew sleepier, an errant thought slipped through his mind. He wished it were Annie that lay beside him, rather than her cat.

* * *

Annie stumbled in the darkness, the storm raging all around her. Wind pulled at her hair and clothing as if in an attempt to rip everything from her body. Her hair was drenched and water ran down her face and seeped into the neckline of her cloak. She clutched Abra tight to her chest, beneath the water-repellent traveling cloak, keeping the cat relatively dry.

Abra trembled every time lightning crashed and thunder boomed, and if Annie didn't have such a tight hold, she was sure the cat would flee in terror. Annie prayed they wouldn't be struck by lightning. If only she could find shelter.

"Go back to the mansion," her inner voice said, but she ignored it.

They neared the moors, and soon Annie would be the tallest entity around, surely drawing the next bolt of lightning. She needed to crouch down and hide among the grass—or something!

Abruptly the storm ceased.

No lightning, no thunder, no wind, no rain.

Only an eerie silence prevailed, somehow more frightening than the storm.

Annie straightened and blinked, slowly looking into the darkness. Over her shoulder she could see warm yellow light from Diamond Hall's windows, beckoning her, telling her to return.

Abra hissed from beneath the traveling cloak. Hair prickled at Annie's nape.

Slowly she turned back to face the moors. . . .

Her heart ceased to beat as a hideous beast rose up from the grass. . . .

* * *

Annie woke with a start. Her heart thumped and she wanted to scream. Her dream world warred with reality, both blending and confusing her as she struggled to place where she was. Gradually, everything came into focus, and she realized she was staring up at a rose-colored canopy and she was in a rosewood four-poster bed.

Not her own simple bed with the brass headboard.

Part of her dream was real then. She was in Diamond Hall . . . and good heavens, she'd given a man fellatio last night.

Annie clapped her hand over her eyes. Her cheeks burned and a warm flush stole through her at the thought of what she'd done, and what he'd done to her, too. All of her mother's rantings came rushing to her mind all at once. How sex of any kind outside of marriage was bad.

But Annie was intelligent and mature. She was living in the new millennium. What made a woman feel wonderful and special was a *good* thing. Not something to be ashamed of.

Gradually, her breathing calmed and she rolled onto her side to look at the fireplace. This time she didn't know whether to scream in terror or shriek in happiness.

There was a very large black-and-white-striped tiger stretched out on the hearth. Even without her glasses she had no problem seeing that he was watching her with intense midnight-dark eyes.

And curled up in a tight ball on the tiger's back was her calico cat.

Abra was sleeping on top of a tiger.

Annie couldn't look away from the tiger's gripping black gaze. A gaze that seemed familiar. On the beast's upper right shoulder, one of its black stripes had a diamond shape in the midst of it, one similar to Karn's tattoo. It occurred to her then that she'd seen a tiger in her painting, before the man had appeared.

That must be it. This tiger is Karn's pet.

She hoped.

Abra blinked her green eyes and stretched her body out along the tiger's back and yawned. She was so tiny compared to the tiger she'd been sleeping on. Annie had the urge to grab a camera, take a picture, then paint the pair of them.

Abra rolled onto her belly and began kneading the tiger's fur with her claws sheathed. A purr rose up within Abra, so loud Annie could hear it across the room.

Annie's heart beat a little faster as she hoped that Abra didn't let those claws out. Her cat would make a tasty breakfast for an irate tiger.

Abra gave another big yawn, then bounded off the tiger. She strolled toward the bed and jumped up, landing on Annie's legs. But there was no doubt Abra was ticked about being left behind. Tail twitching, the cat lifted her nose in the air and pretended she didn't see Annie.

Annie couldn't help but grin. She sat up in bed and scooped Abra into her arms. "I'm so glad to see you, Abracadabra, you little monster." Annie closed her eyes and rubbed her face in Abra's soft fur and smiled when the cat began to purr, obviously forgiving all transgressions.

Well, even if Annie was confused as hell, at least she had her cat.

Something large and hair-covered pushed against Annie's arm. She froze and opened one eye to find herself face to face with the black-and-white tiger.

CHAPTER FIVE

ICE WATER CHILLED ANNIE'S VEINS AS HER GAZE locked with the tiger's black eyes. Her heart pounded and she squeezed Abra so tightly to her chest that the cat stopped purring and gave a strangled *"Mee-owwwrl."*

Both of Annie's eyes were wide. Still holding Abra tightly, she scooted away from the tiger.

But the huge creature started to *change*. And not only did its features morph, it also rose up on its hind legs . . . and shifted into a man. White hair and black stripes changed to skin and long black hair and black clothing . . . to Karn.

Karn was a werewolf! Or make that *weretiger*.

He continued to stare at her with those midnight-black eyes, but Annie went from flat-out scared to good and riled. She released her hold on Abra and the cat stalked away, jumped down, and disappeared under the bed, obviously sulking at the rough treatment she'd just endured.

But Annie crawled off the bed, stood just inches from Karn, and poked her finger at his chest. "You scared the living daylights out of me!" She propped her hands on her hips and glared at the beast of a man.

Karn thought that his kitten was so adorable in her fury that he almost smiled. Annie's brown-sugar eyes sparked with fire and she held her chin high. The way she had jabbed at his chest and shouted reminded him of Abra the previous night . . . how the cat had unsheathed her claws and how her fur stood on end.

So Karn did the only thing he could.

"Don't do that again, you half excuse for a redneck kitty cat—," Annie was saying, when he roughly caught her hair at her nape. Her words abruptly stopped as he held her in a tight grip, not hurting her, but keeping her from moving. She audibly caught her breath just before he pounced and captured her lips with his.

For a moment, she remained stiff, uncertain. Then, like a saber-toothed cat frozen for years in the ice of the Arctic and now finding the sun, she melted into his embrace.

Karn gently bit Annie's lower lip and she moaned. The sensual sound made his cock rigid with lust. He slipped his tongue into her mouth and savored her sweet taste as he enjoyed the smell of her feminine musk and the vanilla scent of the bathing gel.

Her arousal came quickly and easily in response to

his touch, building Karn's own desires beyond his expectation.

Using his free hand to cup her ass, he pressed her tight along his length. She was warm and pliable in his arms, fitting so well in his embrace. And her kiss, the way she tentatively met his tongue with hers made him want her even more. How she nipped at his lip as he had done to her nearly drove him to throw her on the bed and fuck her fast and hard.

It took all his restraint, but he managed to pull away.

Annie's eyes were closed, but then she blinked, looking dazed and flushed. Her lips were swollen from his kiss, her chest rising and falling as though she had just climbed a flight of stairs.

And that chest . . . His gaze lingered on her large, beautiful breasts, so easily seen through the sparkling gold fabric of her nightdress. Without even realizing what he was doing, he slid his hand from her hair to her breast and lightly pinched her taut nub. "Perfect," he murmured as he brought his other hand from her ass up the curve of her waist and cupped her other breast. "My lovely kitten."

Annie sucked in her breath at the feel of Karn rolling both her nipples between his thumbs and forefingers. A mesmerized expression crossed his face, as if he'd never seen a pair of breasts before.

When he lowered his head and licked one of her nipples through the fine material of her nightdress, Annie thought she was going to pass out from the exquisite sensation. Instinctively, she slipped her hands in his dark hair, holding on to him for fear her knees would give out on her. Her pussy grew wetter and she was afraid her juices would be rolling down her thighs if he didn't stop this erotic torture.

Maybe he would take her now, quenching the incredible desire she had for him.

"Like the sweetest berries," Karn murmured as he turned his attention to her other nipple. He gently sucked on it then nipped it lightly between his teeth. Annie gasped and trembled as he eased one hand down, over her hip and to the juncture of her thighs, caressing her mound through her clothing.

She cried out when he slipped his fingers into her wet slit, delving into her creamy folds. It was amazing and so sensual to feel a man's hand between her thighs—definitely better than doing it herself.

He paused for a moment as he murmured, "Tell me if you near climax."

"Karn," she whispered as he continued fingering her and sucking on her nipple. "I'm . . . I'm so close."

He stopped.

As in came to a screeching halt.

Leaving her so on edge and so close she figured she'd come just from one more little suck on her nipple.

But he didn't even touch her. Instead he raised his head and withdrew his fingers from her pussy. While she stared up at him, both dazed and confused, he brought his index finger to her mouth, and said, "Taste your desire for me, kitten."

Annie's jaw dropped out of sheer surprise and embarrassment, and he slipped his finger through her lips.

His dark gaze held hers as he commanded, "Suck."

Her cheeks heated as she obeyed. It was like tasting the forbidden fruit, and that rebellious part of her that had been trying to get out for years now found freedom in the act. Her taste was sweet, rich, and *different*. Different from the taste of his come, and different from anything she'd tasted before.

But what was so sensual was the way he was looking at her as she sucked his finger, as if he was watching her going down on his cock.

"There are rules you need to know, Annie." He withdrew his finger from her mouth and moved it to her nipple as he spoke, taking her away from the brink of orgasm. "We will begin your training this day, and you will learn how to serve my needs."

Huh? was about all Annie could think, with him fondling her nipples and her pussy on fire. She flicked her tongue along her lower lip. "I don't understand. I'm here to find my cousins, not—"

"*Silence.*" The way he said the word brought Annie sharply to attention.

"Who do you think you are to tell me what to do?" She moved her hands to her hips and glared at him. "I'm not a-a servant, or someone you can just order around."

His black eyes burned so hot, like cinders. "Another outburst and you will be punished. This is your only warning."

Annie started to go off on a rant, but snapped her

lips shut. The way he'd said she'd be *punished* . . . Would he really? The only thing she truly knew is that she wasn't sure what he was capable of doing.

"My rules are simple," Karn began as he caught a lock of her hair and twisted it around his fist. "You will obey me without question, and you will refer to me as Sire. You may not achieve climax without my permission, and your goal will always be to please me."

With every one of his statements, his *rules*, Annie's eyes got wider and wider. He was nuts. Crazy even! "You're kidding, right?" She tried to take a step back but he had a tight grip on her hair and one of her nipples. "I don't even know you, and you're treating me like some kind of-of slave."

Karn tugged on the handful of hair he'd wrapped around his fist. "You have earned your first punishment."

He dragged her toward him and kissed her so hard her world spun. When he withdrew from the kiss she felt dizzy and so darn horny she could just about scream.

Wow. Okay. Where were we?

Oh, yeah. The slave thing.

But Karn was moving away from her as she was attempting to gather her thoughts. The trunk lid opened magically, and he withdrew a ruby-red scrap of material and held it up. The thing was so darn sheer she saw completely through it.

"Wear this," he said as he handed the piece of nothing to her. "Beya will be up soon to serve you breakfast. Afterward she will escort you to the gardens."

Annie was tempted to throw the silky cloth at him,

but the look in his eyes and the hard set to his jaw made her think better of it. Instead, she just glared at his backside as he turned away and let himself out of the room.

"You-you, ass!" she hissed under her breath, hurling the minidress at the door.

From beneath the bed came Abra's answering *"Meow,"* and Annie took that as an emphatic agreement.

Annie was positive death by embarrassment was possible as Beya led her through the mansion on their way to the gardens after a nourishing breakfast. The little red dress was sheer enough that it exposed her pink nipples and the curls of her mound. It clung to her full curves as if intent on showing every bit of her body as she passed servants and too many other folks to count. She wished she hadn't put on her glasses, because then she wouldn't so clearly see their interested glances as she walked by with Beya.

Most of the people she passed were fully clothed, but some were dressed as scantily as she was, which made her feel a little better. All of the barely clad women had collars, though, one thing Annie could be thankful she didn't have.

She'd left Abra in her chambers, afraid the cat might get lost in this mausoleum of a mansion. Thankfully, at Annie's request, Beya had come up with a kitty litter box of sorts, along with three crystal dishes for Abra's food, milk, and water.

"Here you be, Mistress," Beya said as she brought

Annie to a pair of double doors at the back of the mansion. The doors were rich mahogany with stained-glass panes in the same intricate design as the diamond on the back of Karn's right shoulder.

Through the red and gold panes, Annie's view was slightly distorted, but she saw what appeared to be extensive gardens. The beauty contrasted sharply with what she'd seen of the mansion in her painting, and in the storm last night when Karn brought her to this world.

"Sire Karn be in the gardens," Beya said as she opened the doors. She gave a nod in the direction of a wall of bright red flowers. "Over yon, Mistress. Behind the starflower blooms."

"Thank you, Beya." Annie took a deep breath and walked away from the tiny woman and out onto a flagstone patio, and then the lush grass. It was wet beneath her feet and her nipples tightened from the slight chill in the air. The rain had stopped late last night. The sky was a broody gray, but she didn't think it would rain now.

Sweet perfume from countless flowers met her nose, like the perfumes of roses and orchids, yet different. Smells of salt and brine, and the familiar sound of waves crashing against the shore filled her senses, reminding her of home.

Massive trees similar to weeping willows surrounded the area like dark sentinels blocking the view of anything outside the gardens. Within its boundaries brilliant flowers in purples, reds, blues, and pinks populated curved paths. Hedges and trees had been shorn into intricate patterns that appealed to her artistic nature. Her fingers itched to hold a paintbrush and to put to canvas the beauty of this place.

She strolled through the wet grass toward the red flower wall, in the direction Beya had indicated. Her heart pounded and she rubbed her sweaty palms on the thin material of the tiny dress. The material seemed to magnify her arousal, rubbing against her taut nipples and gently brushing the curls at her mons.

What Karn had in mind for her, she didn't know. Just the thought of being in his presence made her so hot and horny she couldn't help but imagine what it would be like to have sex with him.

To fuck him. Her cheeks heated at the forbidden word. *That's what Alexi always called it. Fucking. And that's what Karn called it, too.*

When she reached the wall of red flowers, Annie paused for a moment, trying to gain some semblance of composure. *In, out. In, out,* she told herself as she tried to remember how to breathe. It wasn't like she was going to meet some monster, like in her dream last night.

No. Not a monster. A weretiger king with the body of a god and a penchant for ordering women around.

She took a deep breath, rounded the wall, and came to an abrupt stop.

Karn stood beside several pieces of ebony marble furniture with thin veins of gold throughout the smooth polished surfaces. Chairs, a long rectangular table, a bench, and smaller tables were arranged in a private garden area.

The arrogant king was leaning against the flower

wall, his arms folded and his expression stern. But what caught her complete attention was the fact that he was naked.

A mouthwatering, breath-stealing, drop-dead gorgeous hunk of man . . . naked.

And he sported a cock so firm and erect that she almost whimpered with lust at the sight of it.

"You made me wait far too long," Karn said as he studied her.

"Sorry," Annie said automatically, then bit her tongue, wishing she could take it back. She didn't owe him any apologies.

Karn pushed away from the wall and strode toward her. The scars on his chest were more apparent in the sunlight and, like last night, made him seem even darker and more dangerous.

It was then that she noticed the red scarf in one of his hands. She couldn't take her eyes off it until he was standing in front of her . . . and then she was staring at his cock. Such a long, thick, and luscious cock it was, too.

"Look at me, kitten," he demanded.

It was like her body was so attuned to his commands that she reacted at once, tearing her gaze from his erection and focusing on his face. She didn't need her glasses to see up close, and right now she wished she didn't have them on. They made her look frumpy and like a college professor.

Oh, yeah. I am a college professor.

Annie swallowed, tempted to look away from his dark eyes.

Karn folded his arms across his chest. "Remove your clothing."

This time her whole face felt like she'd opened an oven and stuck her head inside. She took a step back, but Karn caught her arm and held her.

Before she had the chance to decide if she was going to do as he asked, or if she would disobey, Karn moved his hands to the neckline of her dress. With one quick tear, he ripped the fragile material. It tore like flower petals in his hands, and the next thing she knew the fabric was sliding off her body and she was completely naked.

Annie gasped and tried to cover her breasts with her hands, but Karn caught her wrists.

He let out a sound like a tiger's growl and her heart dropped to her toes. "You will not hide yourself from me when I wish to see you."

Her brain decided to take a vacation and she didn't know what to say. *Yes, no, maybe so?*

"When you respond you must say, 'Yes, Sire.'" Karn brought up the scarf and slid it over her shoulder and down to her breast. "Is that clear?"

Things were getting a little out of hand, and a little scary. The look in his eyes both excited her and frightened her all at once. It was the fear that made her whisper, "Yes, Sire."

The corner of his mouth curved, a carnal smile that made her clit throb. "Very good, kitten. Now put your hands behind your back and turn away from me."

Strangely enough, it felt almost natural following

his instructions. Not to mention that being naked outside in the middle of a garden felt naughty. Exciting, even. After she put her hands behind her back, Karn guided her by gently pushing her around so that her back was to him.

The next thing she knew he was binding her wrists together with the silk scarf. Her throat went dry and her pulse raced. What was he going to do?

"Kneel," he commanded, even as he placed his hands on her shoulders and applied light pressure, forcing her to comply.

The grass was wet beneath her knees and her long hair slid across her breasts and along the top of her buttocks. Cool air brushed her nipples and mound, causing goose bumps to prickle her skin. With her hands tied behind her back, her breasts thrust forward. Annie didn't know whether to be embarrassed, angry, or excited. She felt a little of everything, and the feelings confused her.

"What are you going to do to me?" she asked as he came around to stand before her.

This time, a short red leather strap was in his hand and large diamond-shaped crystals glittered along its surface.

"You belong to me, Annie." He trailed the strap over her shoulder, up her neck, and along her cheek. "You will wear this collar to make it clear to you and to anyone who sees you."

Her jaw dropped. She stared at him, certain he was out of his ever-loving mind. "I'm not a possession!"

"You are *my* possession, kitten." He smiled and it was so sinfully sexy that all the protests that had been building inside her just melted away. She could hardly think as he fastened the collar around her neck.

Annie couldn't believe she was wearing nothing but a collar and had her hands bound behind her back.

A forbidden thrill shot through her.

Moral indignation and feminist rage aside, she actually *liked* how it felt.

A red leather strap appeared in his hand, and he gently caressed her shoulder with it. "It is time for your first punishment."

Blood pounded in Annie's ears. "You're not going to beat me or whip me, are you?"

Continuing his erotic caress with the strap, Karn slid it over her breasts, teasing her nipples. He moved around to her backside where she could no longer see him and he trailed the strap over her shoulder blades and buttocks. "You will feel both pleasure and pain in your punishment."

"It's the pain I'm not too sure about." Annie's voice trembled slightly. "Karn, I'm scared."

Karn came back around and knelt before her. He placed a light kiss to her forehead then caught her chin in his hand. "I would never hurt you, kitten. Trust me."

CHAPTER SIX

DESIRE ROARED IN KARN'S GUT. HE WAS ALmost crazy with lust at the sight of his woman on her knees, wearing his collar, her hands bound behind her back, her body naked and waiting for him. He inhaled her perfume of vanilla and her woman's musk, drinking it in until he felt as though the intoxicating scent roared through his veins. She was frightened of the unknown, yes, but she was clearly aroused.

He released his hold on her chin and studied her for a moment. With his thumb and forefinger, he pinched the folded leather strap and gently brushed Annie's lips with it. "This time, I will spank you with my bare hand. As I said, you will feel both pain and pleasure." He brought the strap down, lightly touching first one nipple, then the other, and the taut nubs grew harder yet. "Next time I will not be so easy on you, my pet."

Behind her eyewear, Annie's eyes were wide with

concern, but her pupils were large with desire, too. She licked her lips and her voice was husky when she spoke, "I didn't sign up for this. When I followed you through the painting, I came to find my cousins. I've stayed because you're . . . well, so attractive—but even for you, I'm not a toy, or some little child to be ordered around."

Karn slowly shook his head. "I am the King of Diamonds, and you are my mate and future queen. I will never let down my responsibilities to you." As her jaw dropped and her eyes went impossibly wider, he continued, "As such, you must learn to accept my commands, to respect me as a husband and ruler, and to trust me without question."

Annie's thoughts spun. She couldn't believe what Karn was saying. The books she'd read on relationships said zilch about the proper reaction to being told she was going to be spanked by a king, and subsequently informed she was to be the spanker's future queen.

As in marriage?

Bondage?

Slavery?

She shivered, unable to fully comprehend what he'd said. But even harder to believe was the fact that she was so incredibly turned on. Her pussy was hot and wet, her nipples hard in the chill air, her body on fire. She pulled against the bindings at her wrists, but they held tight.

"Before I address your transgressions, kitten," Karn was saying above the pounding in her head, "I wish for you to suck my cock."

As he stood, Annie couldn't help the desire burning through her. Her mouth watered as he held his erection in one hand and pressed it to her lips. With his other hand, he caught a lock of her hair and held her still.

Karn was near to exploding. When she flicked her tongue against the head of his cock, he barely held his groan in check. He pushed his cock into her mouth and she felt hot and wet around his erection.

What a sight that would be, to have Kalina, or perhaps Aleana suckling Annie's nipples. Mayhap both women at once. It would please him greatly to see Annie being so thoroughly pleasured. Naught excited him more than watching his women enjoying one another . . .

Naught except his sweet kitten pleasuring him.

"Enough!" Karn withdrew his cock from between her lips, and it glistened in the sunlight from her wet mouth. "Now for your punishment."

While he helped Annie to her feet, her expression was confused, frightened, yet aroused. "I don't know about this," she said as he led her to the black marble bench beside the wall.

Karn waved his hand, and like magic her bonds fell away. "Take off your eyewear and straddle the bench." His tone was calm but firm. "And do not forget how it is you are supposed to address me."

"Yes, Sire." Annie's heart was pounding like mad as she obeyed. What else could she do? She had always stood up for herself in the academic world, her sharp mind and intelligence serving as weapons that she wielded as easily as a knight might wield a sword. But here . . . she was completely out of her element. She had never been naked with a man, much less done the things she'd done with Karn since only yesterday.

And she didn't understand why a part of her enjoyed this so much. How could she want him even more? Somehow, giving up her power and turning it over to him was exciting, intoxicating even.

After Annie put her glasses on a small table, she straddled the bench. The marble was cool between her thighs and against her pussy and ass. It gave her sharp thrills that curled up and into her belly and made her so hot that for a moment she forgot about the punishment thing. She brought her hands in front of her and braced herself on the bench as she looked up at him.

He slid the leather strap over the marble in front of her. From out of nowhere a blanket appeared, covering the marble. "Lie flat and let your arms hang over the sides."

Annie bit her lip as she held on to the surface that was softened by the cover. She leaned forward until her breasts and mound were pressed flat to the surface. She turned her face so that her cheek was against the bench and she was looking into the garden.

In a matter of moments, Karn had her wrists bound to the bench legs before her, and her ankles tied at the other end. It was driving her crazy how excited and scared she felt all at once.

When she was thoroughly bound, Karn knelt beside her. She could smell his heady male musk and longed to be held tightly by his powerful arms. He gently rubbed his palm over her ass as he watched her face.

"I will only punish you when you disobey me," he said calmly, like they were discussing the day's events over a cup of coffee and a newspaper. "But understand you *will* be punished if warranted."

Annie swallowed hard, fighting down the retort that rushed to her lips, and the niggling of fear that came from his threat. He brought out another red scarf, and the next thing she knew he was sliding it into her mouth, tying it behind her head, and gagging her. The scarf was snug against her cheeks, but not so tight that it hurt.

What is he going to do to me? Her thoughts went wild with images of him spanking her until she cried.

Karn turned to caressing her ass, the feel of his calloused hand making her pussy wetter than before.

The first time he swatted her with his palm she cried out against her gag and tears pricked behind her eyes. Her ass stung, yet it caused pleasure tingles to radiate through her core. Karn continued to watch her face and she found she couldn't take her gaze from his.

He swatted her again and again. First one cheek, then the other, then both cheeks near her thighs, then the top of her ass. The initial shock and pain wore off, and to her surprise she found herself so turned on she was close to climax.

Karn glanced to her buttocks, then back to her eyes as he continued to spank her. "Your ass turns an enticing shade of pink," he murmured as he swatted her again.

Annie groaned, the fire inside her pussy building and building.

"Remember you may not reach climax without my permission." He rested his hand on her tingling butt cheeks. "Are you close, kitten?"

She nodded and he immediately moved away from her and stood. He waved his hand within her line of vision and she was once again free from her bonds, and even her gag was gone. The scarf just plain disappeared. When she raised herself to a sitting position on the bench, her ass burned against its coolness. How bizarre it was to be turned on after being spanked, yet that was exactly how she felt.

After he helped Annie to her feet, Karn led her to the large rectangular table. Once he had covered the table with a cloth, he ordered her to sit at the table's edge, then directed her to lie flat on her back. Again he tied her up. This time her legs were free but her wrists were bound and her arms stretched out and fastened well over her head.

Wind stirred the trees and a gust rushed over her body and her exposed pussy. She heard the sound of the ocean, waves slamming against the shore, driving in again and again. Karn's warm musk surrounded her— the smell of testosterone mixed with something even more wild and primitive.

He knelt between her thighs and her breathing grew more rapid as he scented her mound. In the next moment, he buried his face against her pussy and licked her clit.

Annie's gasp of surprise turned into a moan. He licked and sucked, drawing her close to peak and then backing away, leaving her so frustrated she wanted to scream at him. When he rose up above her, he placed the head of his cock at her core and she caught her breath.

This was it. She was naked and her butt was sore, and now she was going to lose her virginity while strapped down to a table in the middle of a garden. Not to mention the red collar around her neck marking her as his *possession*.

Dang but she wanted him.

Karn's eyes were dark and sensual as he moved the head of his cock slightly into her opening. She bit her lip as she watched him and as she concentrated on the strange but exciting sensation.

He paused with maybe an inch of his cock inside her. Concern was written on his features. "Does that hurt, kitten?"

She shook her head. "Not yet."

Karn held out his palm and in it appeared a red three-dimensional diamond-shaped object that was about the size of an egg. He placed it to her pussy and it began to throb against her clit. No, throb wasn't exactly what it was doing—it felt like the diamond thing was *licking* her clit, too.

Annie moaned, thrashed her head, and shifted her hips. She was coming so close to orgasm that she could barely speak, much less tell Karn that she was about to climax.

As she tried to fight off the orgasm, she felt his cock slide into her a little farther, and yet farther still until he reached the barrier inside.

Her body arched up away from the table and she tried to speak, "Karn . . . Sire . . . I'm going to—"

He cut her off with a sharp demand. "Come for me, kitten!"

Annie's entire body responded to his command. She cried out as the exquisite feelings rocked her body.

At the same time, Karn thrust inside her, tearing past her hymen and burying himself deep in her pussy. Annie gasped as she felt sharp, burning pain, but then she felt only pleasure as he stretched her. Such a full and splendid feeling, unlike anything she could have imagined.

"Did I hurt you?" Karn stopped, his cock fully lodged inside her. He looked even more concerned, and Annie couldn't help a shy smile.

"It feels good." She licked her lips. "*You* feel good inside me."

Karn clenched his jaw and reined in the desire to fuck Annie hard and fast. By the skies, he'd never felt such a need to possess and claim as he did with his future queen.

With a flick of his fingers, he sent the diamond toy back to his chambers using his magic. He then hooked his hands under each of her knees, and held Annie's legs splayed wide so that he could penetrate her more deeply. Slowly, he thrust in and out of her core, and felt her tight channel gripping his cock and rippling with aftershocks of her climax.

She started to close her eyes but he gave her a sharp command. "Watch your king fuck you, Annie. Watch the man who owns you, as he possesses you completely."

Her cheeks were flushed but she looked to where they were joined. She bit her lower lip as she focused on his cock moving in and out of her quim. Karn couldn't take his eyes from her face, and when he saw that she neared climax, he urged her on. "Come, Annie. Climax for me again."

Annie's body rocked and he thrust into her harder and faster. His bollocks slapped against her ass and the sound of flesh against flesh and her small cries filled the garden.

When he came it was with a roar and a triumphant shout. He had made Annie completely his. She belonged to him and *only* him.

Annie actually enjoyed spending the day in the garden with Karn. Every moment with him was sensual and exciting. She liked the deep vibrant sound of his voice, his unusual accent, and even the scars on his powerful chest.

She was constantly aware of her collar but still wasn't sure how she felt about being a *possession*. Good lord, but she was a woman of the new millennium! She had a master's and was working on her PhD, for heaven's sake.

Yet at the same time, she was giddy, excited even, over *finally* losing her virginity. And to a god of a man no less!

After Karn untied Annie's bonds, she heard the voices of Beya and someone else. Annie grabbed the blanket and wrapped it around herself just before they rounded the starflower wall with trays of food in their hands.

Annie thought she would die of embarrassment, for sure this time, while the feast was laid out on the table where Karn had taken her so thoroughly. Thankfully, Beya and the servant soon vanished around the flower wall once the meal had been served. She was also grateful that Karn allowed her to keep the blanket around her shoulders while they ate. It was nippy outside, and the blanket kept her cozy and warm.

Lunch was delicious and her stomach growled in appreciation from just the mouthwatering smells. The food was very different from what she was used to, but she liked it all. There were pastries filled with meat and cheeses, similar to dinner pockets that her mom used to make, yet these had unfamiliar spices and flavors. It was just plain hard to describe.

While they ate, Karn didn't seem to mind answering questions about his realm, as long as her questions weren't too personal. Annie sensed he held his emotions tight inside and she wondered what she'd have to do to get to know him better.

Because amazingly enough, that was what she wanted—to *really* get to know him.

Annie was even able to *finally* get information from him on her cousins. To her amazement, Alice was now the mother of two sets of twins, and Alexi had triplets. That last one was a real shocker. Alexi had never been what Annie would consider the mom-type, but to hear Karn talk, she enjoyed her role as a mother, and as arbitrator of the Kingdom of Spades.

Alexi's spouse however, Darronn the King of Spades, was apparently rather overwhelmed with their three cubs, but as proud as a father could be. Annie could sense Karn's own pride in his nieces and nephews, but he was holding back, not fully letting his emotions show.

Annie couldn't wait to see her cousins and their children, but Karn wouldn't give her specifics. Every time she tried to press him for more information, he would give her the "look" that meant she was headed toward another spanking.

Although she hadn't minded the spanking he'd given her. It still surprised her how erotic the whole experience had been.

The afternoon wore on, and Karn insisted on teaching her more of how to satisfy him. A part of her didn't mind letting him control her. She thought again of what Awai had said, that the submissive had the true control. But rather than revel in that power, Annie felt it was more of a responsibility . . . to pleasure the one who relied on you to please him.

Late in the afternoon, after Karn took her gently in the grass, and after she'd come for at least the tenth time that day, she started shivering from the cold. The sky darkened, clouds swirled above them, and the air smelled of rain. He covered her with the blanket, scooped her up in his arms, and carried her toward the mansion. She was limp with exhaustion, and didn't mind at all being carried.

When Karn took her through the mansion, Annie squeezed her eyes tight and buried her face against his powerful scarred chest as he strode into the building. He was entirely naked and beneath the blanket she was, too. She was mortified that everyone in the castle must know what they had been doing. Karn seemed entirely unconcerned with being seen in his birthday suit, but Annie's whole body flamed with heat and she was sure her face was as bright red as the collar around her neck.

Once they reached her chambers, he took her into the bathing room. Hot water had already been drawn and steam rose from the surface. He tossed aside the blanket, helped her into the pool, and bathed her so carefully that it seemed at odds with his gruff exterior. Inside, Karn was caring and gentle, but instinctively she knew that was something he didn't want known to anyone.

Neither of them spoke while he bathed her. It was just so comfortable being with him.

Besides, what did one say to a man who'd just tied you up, put a collar of ownership on you, spanked you, took your virginity, ate lunch naked with you, and gave you the most amazing orgasms of your life?

After her bath, and after Karn toweled her off, he led her to the bedroom and to the clothing chest. He magically opened it, but this time drew out a nightdress in a pale pink. Again it was made of a sheer material. Annie wanted to protest, yet a part of her enjoyed showing off her body since Karn appeared to enjoy it so much. He didn't seem to care that she was a full-figured gal, and he sure liked how big her breasts were.

She wanted to know what it would feel like to be held in his arms all night, and to wake up with him wrapped around her. "Are you going to stay the night with me?" she asked softly.

"No." Karn caught her chin and held her gaze. "I will see to all your needs, kitten. But it goes no further than my being your Sire, and you learning the art of pleasure."

He slid his fingers down her neck as he released her and then turned away. She watched him leave the room and just stared at the doors after they quietly shut behind him.

A low rumbling noise drew Annie's attention as Abra curled around her ankles. She scooped up the cat and buried her face in the soft calico hair. Tears burned at the back of Annie's eyes as the weight of what he did and didn't say settled inside her.

Karn would see to her physical needs, and he would make sure she was trained in fulfilling his sexual hunger.

But he had no intention of opening his heart and letting her inside. He had no intention of loving her or of being a husband to her, beyond giving her a title and his cock.

CHAPTER SEVEN

THE FOLLOWING MORNING, ANNIE WOKE TO the soft patter of rainfall against her windowpane and Abra snuggled up to her neck. Memories of Karn, the garden, their passion washed over her, and her entire body felt warm at the thought. She was deliciously sore, her thighs and pussy having the ache of a good sexual workout.

Another thing she'd read about and now finally got to experience for herself.

Annie smiled, but it dissolved into a frown as she remembered Karn's parting words from last night: *I will see to all your needs, kitten. But it goes no further than my being your Sire, and you learning the art of pleasure.*

Her thoughts turned toward his earlier statement that she was to be his queen. How could the man simply kidnap her and force her to marry him? Yet, even stranger was how easily she had gone along with everything he demanded of her. Something about him made her want to please him, to be with him. But she hardly knew the man . . . although she certainly knew him well in many ways after yesterday.

With a sigh, she carefully turned on her side and stroked Abra as she looked at the window and watched raindrops make trails down the glass. When she was young, she used to imagine that rain was the sky's tears when its heart had been broken.

While she watched the raindrops roll down the pane, she thought about her childhood. Every time her mother or others had stepped on her heart in her life, she had cried. She never knew her father, and her mother acted as if she hated Annie and resented her very existence.

Annie's grandmother had been a kind and good-hearted woman, and was the only person in Annie's life who showed her any kind of love. But Grandma Travis had passed away close to Annie's tenth birthday, and then she had no one.

It wasn't until she moved away from home to attend San Francisco State University on scholarship, that Annie found true friends and loyal family in her cousins, Alice and Alexi, and in Awai. They had embraced Annie as one of them and had taken her under their collective wings.

She stroked Abra under her chin absentmindedly as she thought about her cousins. Alice and Alexi had been taken away from Annie, and she'd left Awai behind.

Annie moved her hand to her collar and sighed. *And here I am with a man who refuses to love. Talk about irony.*

Sparkles glittered in front of Annie, jarring her from her thoughts. Beya materialized, holding a tray piled high with dishes. Abra scampered off the bed and darted beneath it.

"Breakfast, Mistress," the little woman said as she bustled to a table in the corner of the bedroom. She placed the tray on the table and began arranging items in front of each of the chairs. "Sire Karn will join you shortly."

"Thanks, Beya." Annie slipped out of bed, and then crawled right back under the covers when she realized what she was wearing—the sheer pink nightgown. Her cheeks heated, but the housekeeper didn't seem to notice.

"Come along." As she spoke, Beya carried a crystal dish to the place beside the door where Abra's food and water was kept. "Do not keep Sire waiting."

Annie clutched one of the bedcovers to her chest. "I need to change."

"Rubbish." The housekeeper set the bowl on the floor and rose up to give Annie her no-nonsense look. "You are dressed appropriately for Diamond Hall. You will see," she said and faded into so many sparkles again.

Annie tossed aside the covers and climbed out of bed. Abra peeked out from under the bed and then walked to the crystal bowl of food with her head held high as if she was queen of Annie's New Realm.

With a shake of her head, Annie smiled. But when the handle on the door that led to Karn's room jiggled, she darted right back into bed.

Karn entered her chambers and shut the door behind him. His massive presence filled the room, making even the furniture small in comparison to his large frame. Annie's whole body reacted immediately, her pussy growing damp and her nipples tightening.

He frowned. "I expected you to be waiting for me at the breakfast table, kitten."

Holding her cover tight to her chest, she said, "I didn't get a chance to change."

"I instructed you to never hide yourself from me." His frown turned into a scowl as he strode to the bed and ripped the blanket right out of her hands.

She covered her breasts by folding her arms across her chest, but Karn grabbed her wrists and pulled them away. "You have earned another punishment," he said, with a look so dark that she was surprised into being speechless. He held out his palm and a red strap appeared on it.

In a movement so quick she didn't have time to catch her breath, he turned her on her belly so that she was lying half on and half off the bed. In a matter of a second or two, he had tied her wrists behind her back with the strap.

Annie's face was in the bedcovers and she turned her head sideways so that she could breathe. "Wait. What are you—," she started, then gasped as he moved between her legs and spread her thighs wide. "Karn—"

"Sire," he commanded as he pushed her nightgown up to her waist, exposing her bare ass. "Do you understand why you are being punished, kitten?"

Annie tried to be mad at him, but having him between her legs was making her so hot. She couldn't help
but remember the erotic punishment he had dealt her
yesterday. "You're punishing me for hiding myself . . .
Sire."

Karn caressed her naked flesh and then she felt his
lips and his tongue on her skin and she couldn't help
a moan. She yelped in surprise as he bit her ass, hard
enough that it would probably leave a temporary mark.
Though the bite hurt a little, it surprised her it had been
pleasurable, too.

He rubbed his stubbled cheek over her bare skin
and kissed her crack. Annie moaned, her pussy flooding
with need. When Annie moaned, he murmured, "Remember, kitten, it is about my pleasure, not yours."

"Yes, Sire," she whispered, hoping his punishment
would be as delicious today as it was yesterday.

But instead of spanking her, he picked her up and
set her on her feet, then led her to the table. Her hair
was wild around her shoulders from sleeping on it, and
she felt small and vulnerable next to him.

After he seated her with her hands still behind her
back, Karn took the chair beside her, and moved it close.
"I am going to feed you your breakfast. Do not climax
without my permission."

"Is breakfast that good?" Annie asked, but then he
was sliding a piece of fruit into her mouth at the same
time he moved his fingers between her thighs and stroked
her clit. She jumped from the initial contact and then
moaned around the fruit. It was the same color of red as

a pomegranate and had the consistency of cantaloupe, but tasted like a cross between a mango and an apple.

He bit into a tart then put it to her lips. Annie took a bite just as he thrust two fingers into her core, and she rolled her eyes back from the exquisite pleasure. The strawberry cream cheese taste melted in her mouth as he moved his fingers in and out of her pussy. She pulled against her bonds, wanting to touch him, to hold on to something as he continued his sexual torture.

Throughout their breakfast, he drove her crazy, taking her to the brink of orgasm and then pulling back.

When they had eaten the last of the meal, Karn bent and licked her nipple through the thin material of her nightgown. He continued to plunge his fingers in and out of her pussy.

"Karn . . . I mean, Sire." Annie could barely speak, she was so close. "May I come, please?"

"No." He moved his mouth to her other nipple and kept thrusting into her with his fingers. "You must resist."

"I-I can't."

He only moved his fingers in and out of her faster. "You will not orgasm, or I shall have to punish you."

Annie leaned her head back, her breasts thrust forward and he suckled her nipple harder. "Stop, please," she begged, even though she wanted him to continue and wanted to come so bad she could just scream.

"This pleases me," he murmured as he moved his mouth back to her other nipple. "And you are here to see to my pleasure."

Her thighs began to tremble and a fine sheen of sweat broke out upon her skin. She worked to hold back the impending explosion, though she wasn't completely sure why—except that it would make Karn happy.

Maybe if she made him happy enough . . .

And then he stopped.

Annie groaned as he pulled his fingers out. Just one touch more and she would have come for sure.

"That was your first punishment," he said as he stood. "Your second will come later."

"You're not going to let me come?" Annie muttered, her clit so sensitive that she squeezed her thighs together to try and calm the sensations. "What else am I being punished for?"

"You were not waiting at the table when I came into the room." He stood and pulled back her chair, then helped her stand. "I will deal your consequences to you later."

Annie's gaze snapped up to meet Karn's. "What are you going to do to me, Karn?"

He waved his hand and the tie fell from her wrists. "Do not forget your place, kitten." Then he took her by the elbow and guided her to her trunk. "Always refer to me as Sire, or I may take you to the dungeon."

She swallowed hard, as he opened the trunk with a flick of his fingers. "You would lock me in the dungeon, Sire?"

"Perhaps." He shrugged as if indifferent to the fact that he was suggesting he would lock her up in a cell. "If you earn such treatment."

Annie was quiet as he withdrew a pair of doeskin boots from the trunk that certainly wasn't there when she'd looked before. He also took out a leather dress and a cloak. "Does it bother you to walk in the rain?" he asked as he handed her the leather dress.

She shook her head as she clutched the dress to her chest. "I used to do that all the time at home."

"Good." He frowned at the way she was covering her breasts with the dress. "Put this clothing on."

Annie did as he bade, not wanting to add another punishment to her tally. His dark eyes looked hungry as he watched her slip out of the nightgown and into the dress. When she got it on, she was sure she was going to die of embarrassment, because there were two holes right where her breasts were. Her full breasts poked out like twin torpedoes, not to mention the dress was so short it barely covered her mound.

Karn's feral smile caused Annie to shiver with excitement. As long as no one else saw her in this dress, it actually turned her on to have her breasts on display for him.

He held out his hand, and two white diamond pendants appeared. They looked like earrings, only they had loops at the top of each pendant. Before she could ask him what they were for, he reached up and pinched her nipple, causing her to gasp and the taut nub to grow even harder. He released her, then slipped the looped end of the diamond dangle over her nipple, then slid a golden band up the loop so that the ring was taut. Her nipple turned darker red, almost purple, and the sensation was one of both pain and pleasure.

Annie watched in amazement as he repeated the process on her other breast, then examined his handiwork. It felt exotic to have the charms dangling from her nipples, the loops tight and keeping the nubs erect.

"You will wear these and think of me touching you, tasting you," he murmured as he flicked one of the crystals. "Put on the boots now."

When she bent over to put on the soft leather boots, the diamonds swung and she almost gasped from the sensation of the nipple charms tugging at her as they rocked back and forth. After her boots were on, he held the cloak over one arm, then took her hand and led her out the doors that opened with his magic as they approached.

Panic rose inside Annie as he guided her through the doors and into the hallway. "You're not going to make me walk through the mansion like this, are you?"

He frowned down at her, and Annie was quick to add, "Sire."

"Do not question me," he said as he led her toward the stairs. "Or another punishment will be added."

Annie clamped her teeth together, caught between the urge to rage and the desire to submit.

When they reached the landing, Annie stopped walking, literally digging her heels in. Karn could have used his massive strength to drag her on, or simply have thrown her over his shoulder, but thankfully he didn't.

Karn looked down at his mate, but this time he did not frown. She looked so upset. A key twisted in his heart, unlocking emotions he had not allowed himself to feel in decades. "What is it, kitten?"

She bit her lower lip then took a deep breath. "I can't do this. Punish me if you want, but I can't walk around other people like . . . like this. I didn't mind while we were alone in the bedroom, but I just can't with anyone else."

Annie's voice had trembled as she spoke, and that key in his heart turned a little more. She was such a gentle creature, yet willing to stand up to him if he crossed her boundaries. He did not want to hurt her. Even though he would not allow himself to love her, he could not help but care for his future queen.

Without saying a word, he took the cloak and wrapped it around her, helping her to put her arms through the holes, then fastening it so that it covered her breasts. When he finished he hooked his finger under her chin. "If ever there is something I ask of you that you do not enjoy, then simply tell me. I feel no pleasure in your distress."

He leaned down and brushed his lips over hers, then forced himself to back away and take her hand again.

Annie sighed with relief as they walked down the stairs together. No doubt in Karn's kingdom he was used to his subjects obeying his commands. They probably enjoyed it, even. But the fact that he had listened to her, and cared enough to cover her when she was truly embarrassed and pushed beyond where she would ever want to go, raised her estimation of him even higher.

While they walked together, Karn was silent. The cloak chafed her nipples and the dangles bounced against her breasts, keeping her stimulated. The leather outfit felt exciting the way it held her breasts in the holes, and the way the bottom of the dress brushed her mound as she moved. Even the collar she wore for Karn was a turn-on.

Yet, the walk through the mansion was a little nerve-wracking. What did he have planned for her next punishment? Annie's cheeks burned every time they passed a castle servant. What if they knew what she had on beneath the cloak?

When he took her down a flight of stone steps, deep below the mansion, her heart started to pound like crazy. Odd-looking torches lit the way. Rather than fire, they were glowing orbs on the ends of long sticks held in place by brackets. The place smelled musty and damp, and Annie was sure he was going to lock her up. If he tried, she'd let him know that was another thing she just couldn't handle.

It seemed as if they had walked forever down spiraling steps when they reached a dank hallway. Karn stopped in front of a huge wooden door with an iron handle. With a wave of his hand, the door creaked open, and Annie found herself holding her breath.

It was completely dark as he guided her into the room, and she imagined she heard the scurrying of mice. *Too bad Abra isn't with me. At least I'd have a companion and Abra would enjoy a good chase and a good meal.*

But then again, Karn had told her to let him know if something frightened her. Being locked in a dungeon would definitely qualify as scary.

"Are you frightened, kitten?" he whispered near her ear, as the door closed behind them.

Annie bit her lip. She wasn't really scared with Karn by her side, just nervous about what he had planned for her. "Not as long as you're here."

Karn gave a low purr, telling her that he approved of her choice of words. "You trust me then?"

Strangely enough she did. So far, everything he'd done to her and with her had been pleasurable. Even though he'd locked away his heart, she knew inside that he was a good man, and she did trust him.

In the next instant, a torch lit the room. It took a moment for her eyes to adjust to the light and to see that it was empty, the size of a small bathroom, with a door on the far side.

Relief rushed through her, and then she realized she had no idea what was on the other side of the door. He led her to it and opened it with a wave of his hand.

A gust of moist wind rushed in along with the roar of waves crashing against rocks and sand. Through the doorway she saw a path leading to the shore. They were almost level with the ocean, and it wasn't raining any longer, just a fine mist filled the air.

She shot Karn a look and his lips quirked. "What were you expecting, kitten?"

Annie could tell by the look in his eyes that he'd been teasing her about the dungeon. "So, you do have a sense of humor." She smiled back at him. "I was afraid you didn't."

Karn took her hand and led her down a path through a light mist that wet her cheeks and hair. Through the soft boots she could feel the shale, but it didn't hurt her feet. The air smelled of rain mixed with salt and fish. Seaweed littered the sand near the crashing waves, but it was different from what she was used to. Rather than dark green and brown, it was yellow and orange and made for a colorful shoreline.

The ocean extended for miles and miles, an endless blue-green expanse. They were in a small inlet with massive black cliffs surrounding them and jagged rocks along the beach. She shivered at the thought of falling from those cliffs. No one could survive such a drop.

Thoughts of such an injury made her think of the scars Karn bore. "Where did you get the scars on your chest?" she asked before she could stop herself.

But Karn didn't seem to mind. "From an injury when I was a cub," he said as he raked his hand through his hair, almost feeling again the claws of the jaguar that had nearly killed him. "My brothers and I were foolishly out in the middle of the night when we should have been in bed."

"We all make mistakes, Karn." Annie gave him one of her gentle smiles. "We just have to let go of them and live for today."

Karn gave a grunt, neither agreeing nor disagreeing.

"Do you have any brothers and sisters, other than Alice's and Alexi's husbands?" she asked.

"My youngest brother is Ty." He laced his fingers through Annie's, giving him a more intimate contact with her. "And my sister Mikaela . . . she no longer speaks to the family."

They continued to walk down the shore, and he answered her questions the best he knew how. Whenever the topic became too close to his steel-encased heart, he steered it away.

Annie's hand was small in his grip, and he felt more relaxed than he had felt in an age. "Tell me of your home and of yourself," he said as they kept just out of the reach of the waves pounding the shore.

"Home seems so far away right now." Her brown-sugar eyes seemed distant now, as if she had traveled elsewhere in her thoughts. "I'm a college professor by day, a closet artist by night."

"My mother was an artist." Karn squeezed Annie's hand tighter as he thought about the woman who had raised him, who had loved him, and who had left him when she passed away. "Her name was Elinara."

"I would have loved to have met her," Annie said.

Karn didn't understand why he felt compelled to tell her about those he had loved and lost. Perhaps it was to make sure she understood why he would not love again. "My mother died many years ago of the magical fever that took my father and my betrothed, Ima, as well. It was their fault that they caught the fever. They fooled with magics they had no business disturbing."

"I'm sorry." Annie squeezed his fingers in return and her eyes told him how deeply she meant it.

He shrugged, stuffing away the feelings that no longer mattered. What was done was done, and he had learned to steel his heart long ago. "What of your father and mother?" he asked.

She sighed and gave a sad smile. "I never knew my father, and my mother often said she wished I'd never been born. My only real family are my cousins Alice and Alexi and my aunt Awai."

Karn came to a stop and pulled Annie into his arms. He brushed his lips over her forehead. "I also feel sorrow for your losses, kitten."

"I'm okay." She looked up at him and pressed her body against his. "Do you understand why it's so important for me to see my cousins? To make sure they are alive and well?"

"Yes." He brushed a strand of hair from her eyes. "You will see them, soon."

Karn truly could not help himself as he moved his lips to hers and gently kissed her. At the back of his mind he knew that if he was not careful she would expect more of him than he was willing to give . . . more than he *could* give.

They continued walking together, hand in hand, both silent.

Annie's heart ached for Karn and the loves he had lost, and she wished there was some way she could help heal his heart.

Wind tossed her hair and moist, salty air brushed her face. The ocean roared as waves broke against the shore and a shrill call like that of seagulls filled the air.

But when she looked up, the birds were green and blue with brightly colored faces like parrots.

When they reached a small cove, Karn pulled Annie near the smooth rocks and drew her into his embrace. She gasped as he slid his hands beneath her cloak and palmed her bare breasts. It was exciting having him touch her like he was, out on the beach.

Karn felt the nipple rings and his mate's engorged nubs and his cock hardened. "I must have you," he said as he brushed his lips over hers. "Now."

Annie's cheeks were flushed, her eyes glazed with desire. "Yes, Sire."

Her willingness to call him Sire when she was aroused almost made him roar with pleasure. He led her to one of the smoother boulders in the cove and removed her cloak. After he tossed it onto one of the smaller rocks, he commanded, "Stand in this spot, put your hands against the boulder, and widen your thighs."

Trembling with excitement, Annie turned around and braced her palms against the flat rock. He had ordered her to stand just far enough from the boulder that she was bent at the waist. Cool, moist air chilled her breasts and her ass, too.

Karn pushed her dress up over her hips, fully exposing her butt cheeks. "No one will see us, right?" she asked. Somehow the thought both excited her and scared her.

"No one, kitten," he said, and she felt the soft caress of a leather strap over her bared flesh. "It is time for your punishment. Do you remember why you are being punished?"

Annie swallowed. She wasn't sure she liked the idea of him using a strap this time. What if it hurt? She would tell him to stop, and he would, she was certain. "Yes, Sire," she said. "For not being at the breakfast table when you came into the room."

"Very good. You should never deny me pleasure that is mine by right, and spending time with you when I wish it is a pleasure indeed."

She heard the rustle of leather, then felt the head of his cock against her entrance. Annie was still aching from needing to come earlier. What if she came without permission? How would he punish her then?

Karn drove his cock into her core and she didn't have time to think any longer. All she could do was feel. God, he stretched her, filled her, making her whole body shiver.

She felt the first lash as he started moving his cock in and out. The lash was light and didn't even sting. He continued thrusting into her pussy, and drawing back out again in slow, even strokes as he lashed her ass again and yet again.

"Your skin is a lovely cream color," he murmured. "It pleases me how your ass turns pink from the strap while I fuck you."

The sensations were wild. Pain mixed with a sort of bliss that made her arch herself up higher to take more of the sexual punishment. Mist continued to fall on her backside, her hair, her cheeks. The roar of the ocean blended with the sound of the strap striking her again and again. From being engorged with the tightened nipple rings for so long, her nipples ached and throbbed, which mingled with the pleasure and pain Karn was inflicting on her.

Closer and closer she came to orgasm until she was there, standing on the precipice as though on the edge of one of the surrounding cliffs. "May I come, Sire?" she asked, barely able to speak while he was driving his cock in and out of her pussy and whipping her.

"Hold," he commanded, slapping her a little harder with the strap.

Annie yelped and almost came, but his confident instruction kept her from exploding.

"Now, kitten," he shouted. "Climax for me *now.*"

A different kind of orgasm took hold of her. One that seemed to radiate from her pussy like ripples in a pool of water. Small at first, then larger and larger until it filled her from head to toe. Her body shook and trembled against Karn's body.

Vaguely, she was aware of his shout and then his warm come filling her core. He leaned against her back and wrapped his arm around her belly. Annie sighed, enjoying the feel of his muscular body as he held her, loving the feel of his cock still inside her.

Annie knew it was too late for her. Karn might not want to love her, but she was falling in love with him.

CHAPTER EIGHT

ANNIE PERCHED ON THE CUSHIONED WINDOW seat in her chambers, her arms wrapped around her bent legs, her chin on her knees, and Abra curled up on her toes. It had been raining all day and she and her cat had been confined to their room. Karn hadn't come to see her yet today and Annie missed him.

Likely Abra did, too. Annie sniffed. "Traitorous cat," she murmured as she pushed her glasses up the bridge of her nose. The little beast seemed rather smitten with the dark and brooding man.

Not unlike her mistress.

It was shadowed and gloomy outside, matching Annie's current mood. Inside, the fire crackling in the hearth kept the room warm, but she could feel the chill from outside radiating through the windowpanes.

Annie had actually lost count of the passing days. Had it been two weeks, or maybe three? Every day, Karn spent a few hours with her, teaching her countless ways of pleasuring him. In turn, he fulfilled almost all her sexual fantasies and introduced her to things she'd never dreamed of.

She wore his collar all the time, but he only had her wear the nipple rings on occasion. They added to the erotic play, and she really didn't mind calling him Sire when they were enjoying sex together. She was glad he didn't insist on her referring to him as Sire when they were in public. Ever since the day she had let him know how much it bothered her to be seen in a state of undress in front of others, he'd been much more aware of her feelings and needs, as if he had an extra sense.

"I can't get enough of him," she murmured, and her warm breath fogged the beveled glass pane closest to her.

Today, though, she was stir-crazy, wanting to be outside enjoying the nonexistent sunshine and good hard sex with Karn. At the thought of him, she brought her fingers to the red collar that marked her as his possession. Why did it feel so comfortable, and why did she actually like it?

God, I'm addicted to him. His touch, his smell, his body, his cock . . .

But what really attracted her to Karn was his intelligence, his dark and sensual nature, and the times he rewarded her with a slight smile.

Yeah. The smile curls my toes.

The more time she spent with Karn, the more she grew to admire him as a man and as a king. He ruled gently but firmly, and even though he didn't show it, she knew he cared deeply for his subjects. She wondered if the villagers realized that.

Annie's fingers lightly caressed the diamond-shaped crystals on her collar as she thought about their most recent excursion just days ago. Karn had taken her through the village and she'd seen the amazing sights that she still couldn't get used to, such as machines that operated by magic and carts moving without horses or motors. If a man was building something and ran out of nails, all he'd have to do was hold out his palm and a handful of nails would appear, seemingly out of nowhere. On a previous trip to the village, Karn had explained to Annie how he and his people were able to manipulate matter along with a good dose of psychic energy.

Even for a college professor with multiple degrees, the concept was mind-boggling.

The admiration the villagers had for Karn was obvious in the way they spoke to him, and her appreciation for him grew even stronger. His subjects treated their king with a kind of reverence. Not like an old friend, but as a mentor and someone they respected greatly, yet feared, too.

The villagers had responded to Annie's warmth, to her questions, and to her interest in their lives and their work. She had the feeling that she could give them what Karn couldn't or wouldn't . . . heart and soul and love.

Annie moved her hand from her collar to pick at the hem of her ruby-red minidress. It was another one of those snug and sexy outfits that she had grown used to wearing, but it was a little more elaborate and risqué than her other dresses. Its neckline plunged so low that a good portion of her breasts showed. It molded itself to her full curves, and it was backless all the way down to the crack of her ass. Beya had brought it to her earlier, explaining that Sire Karn wanted her to wear it today.

What's he up to this time? Maybe he'll tear it off me like he did the first time we made love.

Well, the first time we had sex, that is.

She sighed and wiggled her bare toes beneath Abra's weight. The cat simply yawned and stretched, then went back to resting. Annie smiled, but then it faded as she thought of her cousins. It frustrated her that Karn wouldn't take her to see Alice and Alexi, but when she pressed the matter, he punished her. She actually enjoyed the punishments, but she didn't seek them out. Although she'd been tempted . . .

She pressed her nose and forehead against the fogged pane and the cold seeped under her skin and caused her nipples to harden.

Would Karn be coming soon for her?

Annie had met several of the people who worked in Karn's mansion, mostly in passing, but for the most part Karn kept her to himself. He never let her spend time alone with anyone but Beya. Even then, Beya only came in long enough to serve her meals before she disappeared.

And Beya really did just that. She could vanish into thin air, leaving sparkles in her wake that would twinkle and then disappear. Annie smiled. Beya was kind of like a fairy godmother or something.

A knock at the door jarred Annie from her thoughts, and she swung her legs down. At the same time, she almost knocked Abra off the window seat. The cat glared at Annie, then gracefully jumped down and vanished under the bed to sulk.

Annie couldn't help but smile as she walked across the room and opened the door. When it swung open she stepped back in surprise at the sight of two drop-dead gorgeous women.

Both wore nothing but red collars, nipple charms, and twin smiles.

"Such a fair one," murmured the stunningly beautiful woman with dark eyes and skin the color of a raven's wing. A single white lock highlighted her features, traveling from her forehead, down to her shoulders. "I am Aleana."

"And I am the sorceress Kalina." The woman with brilliant amber eyes and black hair took Annie's hand in hers. "You will make a lovely queen."

Annie was too unsettled to say anything other than, "Er, thanks." She had a hard time not staring at their perfect bodies, beautiful breasts, and shaved mounds. For some reason, the sight of their naked bodies caused a tingle in her pussy that radiated up into her belly.

Her cheeks heated as she blurted out, "Why aren't you wearing anything?"

Aleana shrugged and Kalina said, "We enjoy the freedom." The sorceress tugged at Annie's hand. "Come, or we shall be late to the tea party. Sire will not be pleased if we keep him waiting."

At the thought of Karn erotically punishing Aleana or Kalina, a rush of jealousy seared Annie's veins. It came as no surprise to her, though. She'd already come to accept the fact that he meant more to her than a casual sex partner.

She was in love with him.

Unfortunately for her, it was clear Karn didn't feel the same way.

Karn paced the tea room, his jaw set and his mood even more sullen than normal. Lord Kir, his friend and guest, was watching Karn with an amused expression on his strong features.

A low growl rumbled in Karn's chest. Just the thought of Annie made his cock spring to life, and he ached to thrust it into her quim. Ever since he had drawn Annie into his world, he could not get enough of her. He felt the fierce need to protect her and had no desire to bed any other women, or to share Annie in any way.

Today that would change. He had planned the *da'mea,* a "sharing tea," to return to the ways of his people, and to watch his future queen being pleasured.

Kir, lord of Emerald City and of the mountain wolf clan, leaned one shoulder against the wall and folded his arms across his chest. "You have fallen for the maid," he stated as if it were fact. "You are in love with her."

"No." Karn's response came out as a growl and he

paused his pacing and shot Kir a dark look. "She is naught more to me than a willing wench who will serve as my queen."

"Sire," Kalina said from the doorway behind him.

Karn turned and his attention immediately shot to her, only to see Annie beside the sorceress, hurt glistening in her eyes.

And yet, Annie stood between Kalina and Aleana, her chin high. His kitten was so beautiful his heart ached, but the pain in her brown-sugar eyes caused a knot to form in his gut. Obviously, she had overheard his callous words.

For a moment, he battled regret. Then, with a sigh, he decided fate had done him a favor.

Better she know now.

"You kept me waiting." He kept his expression stone hard as he gestured to the low tea table, surrounded by large black velvet cushions. "Be seated."

Tears threatened to well up in her eyes, but she wasn't about to let Karn see how much he'd hurt her. She kept her head up and avoided his gaze as she moved toward the low table set for eight. Her face felt frozen and her heart just as cold after overhearing the tail end of what Karn thought about her. She had hoped he would grow to love her, but obviously that had been an empty hope.

The low rectangular table was the centerpiece of the room, but there were also decorative tables, and black vases with gold inlay that were filled with red flowers. On the walls were three majestic oil paintings in rich wooden frames of burnished gold. The pictures were all stormy seascapes that went well with the room. Despite her hurt at Karn's words, her artistic sensibilities were attracted to the incredible detail in the paintings. If only she had her art supplies, she could at least lose herself in her work until she saw her cousins again.

Kalina and Aleana seated Annie between them on one side of the table, as if protecting her. The cushions were large and Annie's molded to her body as she sank into it. Like the other women, she sat cross-legged. The minidress hiked up to Annie's hips, almost exposing her mound, and cool air brushed her bare folds.

It was then that she noticed the gorgeous man leaning with one shoulder against the wall. The man's chest was as bare as Karn's, and just as broad and muscular. He had sapphire-blue eyes, golden-blond hair to his shoulders, tanned skin, and his breeches were tight, molded around the thickness of his cock. Obviously, he was turned on.

No doubt by Kalina and Aleana.

Certainly not by me, Annie thought as she clenched her hands on the cloth-covered table and continued to ignore Karn. *I can't even interest the man who's been screwing me. What does that say?*

The golden-haired man pushed away from the wall and sauntered toward them. In a slow and athletic movement, he seated himself on the opposite side of the narrow table, directly across from Annie. Openly, he appraised her and gave an untamed smile, as if approving of her curvaceous figure.

He reached over the table, took her hand from where it was resting, and raised it to his lips. "I am Kir," he murmured, his deep voice sexy and vibrant. "Lord of Emerald City and the mountain wolf clan."

"I'm Annie." She did her best to give him a little smile. "Lady of naught."

Lord Kir brushed his lips over her knuckles and heat rushed to Annie's cheeks. "If you were my Lady, you would be the most cherished woman in my realm."

A low growl rumbled from where Karn was still standing, and Annie was sure her face was stoplight red. *Let him stew,* she thought, despite the twinge of embarrassment. Without looking at Karn, Annie held Kir's hand just a moment longer, and then slowly let her fingertips slide from his.

Out of the corner of her eye, she saw Karn's thunderous expression and she barely kept from smiling. Apparently, he wasn't into sharing his *possession* with other men.

She pushed her glasses up the bridge of her nose, settled her hands in her lap, and studied the intricate designs on the black china plates and teacups. Like the stained-glass doors leading to the garden, the red and gold diamond pattern matched the one on Karn's shoulder.

While Annie remained quiet, Kalina and Aleana chatted easily with Lord Kir. From the sensual tone of their conversation, it was obvious they were *very* familiar with him. While they talked, Annie absently raised a hand to her collar and rubbed her finger over one of the diamond-shaped crystals. The collar felt confining now instead of comfortable. If she wasn't concerned that Karn would erotically punish her in front of everyone, she would yank it off and throw it at the jerk.

Laughter and conversation came from the doorway, and Annie glanced up to see three people appear in the room—two men and a woman—and the air sparkled around them. They were all only as tall as Beya, perhaps three feet in height. One of the men wore a very large and peculiar orange head covering that reminded Annie of a goofy version of an old-fashioned stovepipe hat.

The other man had a pinched face and a haughty expression. He rather looked like a snobbish mouse—all he needed was whiskers instead of his neatly trimmed mustache.

Appearing behind the men was a cute and perky-looking woman in a light blue dress. She had a fresh and beautiful smile, and her hair tumbled over her shoulders in golden-blond ringlets. She gracefully sat on one of the cushions beside Kir and gave him a reverent nod. Mouse-man sat on the other side of Kir, and goofy-hat-man sat at the end of the table.

Annie was intensely aware of Karn as he seated himself opposite hat-man, on the only remaining seat cushion, but she still couldn't look at him.

She was also incredibly aware of the two naked women to either side of her, and how comfortable they seemed to be in their nakedness. Annie's clothing was revealing, but at least she *had* clothing.

"I'm Lia," said the blond woman as she extended her hand and smiled as Annie took it. "We are Munch-folk from near Lord Kir's realm." She released Annie's fingers and gestured toward hat-man. "That is Derk, our mayor." And then she pointed to mouse-man. "Ront, our constable."

Both men nodded to Annie and said almost as one, "A pleasure, Milady."

"A pleasure." Annie returned their nods and tried to keep her face straight. In her mind was a vision of *Alice in Wonderland*'s tea party, and the thought almost brought an absurd giggle to her lips.

Beya appeared with a tray full of pastries and cookies, along with a tall teapot, a bottle of what looked like oil, and a bowl of starflower petals that she set before Karn. In just a matter of moments, everyone had been served and tea poured into the teacups.

"Enjoy the sharing tea," the sprightly woman said with a wink before vanishing into so many sparkles.

Before they started eating the goodies, Karn retrieved a small votive-sized candleholder with his magic. Once he set it on the table, he placed the bowl of red starflowers atop it, then poured in oil that smelled of cinnamon and spice. After he lit the candle with his magic, he stirred the oil and starflower petals.

Almost immediately the sweet smell of the blooms and spice filled the room, and Annie instantly relaxed. All tension in her body faded, and for the moment she no longer felt any of the pain that had been in her heart since she heard Karn's words.

Between the delicious treats and good conversation, the "sharing tea," as Beya had called it, was actually quite enjoyable.

The cookies tasted like chocolate mint and the pastries, which were filled with exotic fruits that tasted as though they'd been fermented, warmed Annie's belly. The tea itself had an unusual taste to it, like a mixture of licorice and caramel, and its warmth added to the slow burn in her stomach and the slightly woozy feeling in her head.

Annie hiccupped and clapped her hand over her mouth, but no one seemed to notice. Between the starflowers and tea, she felt so relaxed and uninhibited, like she could try anything in the world.

By the time the Munchfolk took their leave and vanished in a glittery puff, Annie was feeling positively delicious and so horny she didn't care if Karn did just consider her a willing lay. Her nipples were hard and aching and her pussy tingled. She found herself staring more and more openly from Kalina to Aleana and back. One of her deepest fantasies had involved a threesome with another woman, and right now she was loose enough to try it.

Karn waved his hand in a dismissive gesture and the table, dishes, and leftover food vanished. Only the two men and three women and the cushions they were sitting on remained.

"Relax," Kalina murmured near Annie's ear, the feel of the sorceress's breath against her cheek sending delicious shivers throughout Annie. The next thing she knew, she was partially reclined back against the cushion and Kalina was lightly circling her nipple through the thin material of her dress. Aleana took Annie's glasses and laid them on a corner table.

Kalina slid her finger down the curve of Annie's breast. "The *da'mea* tea will only enhance the desires that already exist within your heart and soul." Annie caught her breath as the sorceress slid her finger near Annie's mound. "Have you always wanted to enjoy a woman's pleasures, along with a man's?" Kalina asked.

"Yes." The word came so easily to Annie's lips that it surprised her.

"Good." The sorceress smiled. "That is the purpose of a sharing tea. To share one's mate."

So that's what this was all about—Karn wanted to share her.

Although if he intended to screw one of these women she'd kill him. Right after she fucked him.

But first she intended to drive him out of his mind.

"I have fantasized about being with a woman while a man watched." Annie turned to look at Karn as Aleana lowered her head and flicked her tongue across Annie's still clothed nipple.

The look on Karn's face nearly caused her to smile. This time she could read his gaze and she could see deeper into what truly lay in his soul. It was turning him on to watch the women touch her, but at the same time it was driving him mad.

Even though he'd said what he did, he still wanted her for himself.

Lord Kir let out a low rumble of satisfaction as Kalina and Aleana stroked Annie's body. Annie gave herself up to the sensations of the women touching her. It satisfied her immensely to know that it was driving Karn mad to watch the women, and to have another man watching them, too.

Kalina's small fingers slipped between Annie's thighs. The sorceress lightly kissed Annie and stroked her clit. Kalina's lips were soft and her touch so sensual. She tasted of tea and the sweet flavor of the fruited pastries.

Annie's head spun from the kiss and from the *da'mea* tea, but it wasn't like being drunk at all. It was more relaxing, and her mind and thoughts felt freed from all societal restrictions.

While Kalina kissed her, Aleana slid the fine material at Annie's neckline aside, freeing her breasts. The beautiful woman flicked her tongue over Annie's nipple, causing her to arch her back and moan. Kalina gave a soft purr and moved her mouth to Annie's other nipple.

Annie's dress was up around her hips and both women were stroking her pussy now. Kalina fingered Annie's clit while Aleana thrust three fingers into her core. She was so close, so close to coming.

"Remember, you cannot climax without Sire's permission," Kalina murmured.

But Annie didn't care. Her eyes were heavy-lidded but she saw both men watching—and both were now naked, their cocks standing at rigid attention like military sentinels. Lord Kir had a fierce and predatory expression while Karn clenched his jaw and looked ready to tear the place apart.

As Annie neared climax, Karn's dark gaze met hers. She didn't ask permission first. The hunger and jealousy in his eyes threw her over the edge into a powerful orgasm. Heat flushed her from head to toe and her body rocked against the women's mouths and hands.

Karn had never felt such desire, lust, and fury all at once. He could only fault himself for arranging the tea and sharing Annie, for trying to force himself back to a place where Annie meant less than she did—but he'd be damned before he would let Lord Kir near his woman.

Even as Annie's body still quaked from her climax, Karn glared at Aleana and Kalina. "See to Lord Kir's needs," he ordered.

Both women slipped away from Annie and immediately went to Kir.

Karn moved to Annie's side and growled. She kept her face away, ignoring him. He growled again, moved between her thighs, and caught her face in his hand. He was determined that she would know to whom she belonged. "Look at me, kitten," he demanded. "Watch me fuck you."

Her brown eyes were wide as he thrust his cock into her core and held still. She gasped as she stared up at him, her body trembling beneath his.

Behind him he heard the sounds of sex from Kir and the women, soft moans and sharp cries.

Karn focused his entire attention on Annie. "You are mine, kitten." He growled and was tempted to release his *tigri* pheromones to ensure she would scream with need for him. "No one is ever to touch you again." He gritted his teeth. "Do you understand?"

Annie seemed to struggle with herself for a moment.

Karn expected a lash from her tongue, full of anger for his insulting words earlier. He steeled himself, trying to decide about punishment versus silent acceptance—but even as he watched, Annie's face changed.

It was as if she had squeezed her anger into a fine diamond, then released the hardness, leaving only light radiating from the soft lines of her face.

She writhed beneath him as though trying to take him deeper. "I understand you," she whispered. "And I need you, Karn."

Stunned, intrigued, he began moving his cock in and out of her tight channel. While he fucked her, he sucked on first one nipple, then the next. Annie cried out with one orgasm, then another, but still he drove her on. He wanted her to remember only the pleasure *he* had given her and none other.

"I can't take any more," she said, her voice trembling from yet another orgasm.

"You can and you will." Karn increased his strokes, his bollocks slapping her ass as he fucked his woman even harder.

His eyes locked on Annie's—

The orgasm that slammed into him took him by complete surprise. He hadn't intended to climax yet, but the way she was looking at him drove him over the edge. A roar rushed from his chest and his bellow filled the room as his come filled her core. She came again, her soft cry making his orgasm even more powerful.

When he had emptied himself into Annie, Karn scooped up her limp body and held her tightly to his chest. Without a backward look to the man and women still in the tea room, he exited and carried Annie through the mansion, up the staircase, and to her room.

His jaws hurt from clenching his teeth. His muscles felt banded, and his heart ached and rattled in his chest. Such sensations distressed and angered him.

He was losing control of himself.

Something he absolutely could not . . . would not . . . *must* not do. Not now, and not ever. A childish part of him wanted to blame Annie, but he knew where the true fault lay. Even more, he knew whose responsibility it was to regain that safe, careful control.

After all, his will protected Annie as well as himself, didn't it?

Besides, our time together has become too distracting. I am a king first, above all things, loyal to my realm and my brothers. Yes. It is too distracting. Problematic, messy, dangerous—I will only break her heart, hurt her worse than I did today.

Distance was the only answer.

Karn knew he had to put space between himself and his future queen.

CHAPTER NINE

KARN WAS GONE.

When Annie woke the day after the tea party, Beya had informed her that he'd left and the housekeeper hadn't known when the king would return.

That was two Tarok days ago, and Annie was miserable. Today, she was wandering through the mansion, its shadows and darkness only adding to her bleak mood. She was wearing the most conservative clothing she could find, which happened to be one of Karn's black shirts. Even though she had a generous figure, his shirt was so big on her that it fit like a dress, but was far more concealing than any of the sheer outfits in her trunk.

The only problem was the shirt smelled like him, the warm musky scent making her heart break just a little more.

After the "sharing tea," she'd fallen asleep, alone in

her own bed once again, but hoping Karn had realized he did care for her.

So much for hope.

Where had he gone? She hadn't seen Kalina since he left, and a part of her felt sick inside at the thought of the sorceress sharing his bed. It may be the way of his world, to have a mistress or two, but it would never be a part of hers.

Annie trailed her finger along the dark wood-paneled wall in a section of the mansion she hadn't explored yet. It was darker in this wing, with no candles burning in the wall sconces. A large window was at the end of the hallway, but with the constant dreary rain outside, only gray light spilled into the corridor.

As she walked along the flagstone-tiled hallway, Annie made no sound at all. The tiles were cool beneath her bare feet and she wished for the thousandth time that she knew where her clothing was. She could sure use her jeans and her own T-shirt.

Yesterday, Beya had told Annie this wing was an unused portion of the mansion, but Annie still knocked before opening each door to peek inside. She'd seen several bedrooms, all with dustcovers over the furniture, hiding whatever lay beneath them. She'd also come across a room with fine swords, daggers, and lances displayed on its walls, and it had a couple of leather packs in it that were similar to the backpacks she used to cart her books in while she was going to college.

When she reached the end of the hallway, she peered through the pane and saw a magnificent view of the ocean at the foot of the black cliffs. Like in her painting of the mansion, waves pounded the imposing cliffs in a relentless battle of water versus stone.

The memory of her walk along the beach made her heart ache even more. She turned her thoughts to the great body of water that reminded her of home. After Karn had taken her with her hands braced against the rocks, they had walked along the sand barefoot. She had been delighted that the water was warmer than the cold ocean around San Francisco.

A knot twisted in her belly as she watched wave after wave crash against the cliffs. Surprisingly, she had enjoyed her stay at the mansion, up until the sharing tea. Now she was homesick, missing Awai, her apartment, the classes she taught, and her art. Most of all, she missed her cousins.

Several times Annie had considered leaving the mansion and searching for her cousins on her own. The only thing that made her nervous about the journey was the stories she'd been told about the marsh. Likely, the tales of a marsh monster were meant to intimidate and to keep her from leaving the mansion. Other than the boggy-man stories, no one seemed to want to give Annie any information about much of anything at all, and it was driving her crazy.

But what was driving her the most insane was the way that her body craved Karn's touch.

Annie closed her eyes. She could see so clearly his strong angular jaw, the passion in his ebony eyes, his large muscled frame and powerful chest. Even the scars across his chest made him that much more striking. She shifted, causing the tunic she was wearing to rub against her nipples and she bit her lip to hold back a moan.

Her pussy ached and her core flooded with need. She brought her hands to her nipples and pinched the already hard nubs. As she imagined Karn's mouth upon her breasts, Annie eased her fingers beneath the tunic and cupped her mound.

She could almost feel the bonds on her wrists and ankles as Karn tied her to the bed, spreading her body out for his pleasure. Her fingers eased into her slit as she pictured Karn's head between her legs, his stubble rasping the soft skin around her pussy in contrast to his soft wood brown hair sliding over the inside of her thighs.

Annie dipped two fingers into her core then spread her juices over her clit. Slowly, she started fingering herself, imagining Karn's tongue upon her pussy. And when he'd bring her close to peak, he would rise up and thrust his cock into her core. She would struggle against her bonds, loving the feel of them tying her down, yet wanting to grab him and hold on while he rode her hard.

His expression would be fierce, his eyes blazing with passion. Annie felt her climax building and building as she remembered his touch, the way he looked at her and made love to her.

In her mind she was waiting for him to give her permission to come . . . thinking of him driving into her, harder and faster as she clung to her last thread of restraint. She imagined his shout of "Now, Annie! Come for me, kitten!" and it threw her over the edge.

The orgasm rushed through Annie. Her hips moved against her hand and she continued to circle her clit, drawing out every last wave until the sensations were too much to go on.

She slipped her fingers from her pussy and brought her hand to her nose and breathed in the rich scent of her juices. If only the smell of Karn's semen was mixed with the scent. It was a rich, heady smell that she'd grown to love.

With a sigh, Annie braced her forehead and both palms against the windowpane. The pane was cold against her skin, helping to chill her lust for Karn. Her breath fogged the view as she looked out into the dreary afternoon, and in turn her glasses clouded over.

Annie removed her glasses and cleaned them with the bottom of Karn's tunic while she stared at the ocean.

Something dark moved along the cliff's edge, high above the rocky shore. *A two-headed something?*

Frowning, Annie slipped her glasses back on, but whatever was out there was gone.

A shadow. That's all it was.

Shaking her head, Annie turned away from the window and moved to the massive mahogany chamber door to her left. She knocked, waited for a moment in case someone was in the room, and then gripped the door handle. The large pewterlike handle felt cold in her hand, and for a moment she had to struggle with it to open the door. When it finally gave in to her efforts, the hinges creaked, sending a momentary chill down her spine.

Annie squinted into the darkness. As her eyes adjusted to the dim room, dark forms gradually came into view, and Annie almost screamed. She wasn't exactly the screaming type, but she was so excited she could hardly contain herself.

She'd discovered an art room.

Three easels occupied the center of the chamber, canvases were stacked against the walls, and countless other artist treasures filled the room. For the first time since before the sharing tea, Annie felt a burst of pure happiness. Art had meant so much to her before she was taken from her home, and the need to create was a part of her very soul.

Annie spent the day exploring the room, righting pictures that had fallen down and organizing the painting supplies she found. There were empty canvases, tubes of oil paints, a box of pastels, some kind of cleaner that smelled more like almonds than turpentine, and a box of ebony-handled brushes with bristles made from fine silver, gold, and bronze hair, probably from the horselike beasts she'd seen in the village that were called *jul*. There were also countless canvases of portraits and landscapes, obviously created by an artist with true talent.

"Karn's mother," she murmured as she moved to a painting of a beautiful white castle that sparkled in the sunshine, with acres of gardens in every color of the rainbow spread out before it. "He mentioned she was an artist." She checked the corner and saw the ornate initials, Q.E.

Queen Elinara.

The room was rather dusty, telling Annie it had been awhile since its contents were used, but the supplies were in fabulous condition.

In this magic place, everything is probably enchanted, she thought as she arranged the oil paints. They were in tubes that looked as if they were made from oilskin, and she found a palette made from rosewood in the shape of a paw print with wells where each pad would be. The pastels were in compartments on a long wooden tray that had a snug-fitting wooden lid, and the lid was inlaid with a heart, a spade, a diamond, and a club.

Annie smiled. She felt like a giddy child who'd been searching for the end of the rainbow and had found her pot of gold.

After searching out a castle servant, Annie was provided with the tools she needed to give the room a good spring cleaning.

Well, maybe a winter cleaning, in this bleak place, but a cleaning nonetheless.

Late in the evening, once she'd tackled most of the room, Beya tracked Annie down. The woman appeared in her usual manner—out of nowhere—scaring the crud out of Annie in the process.

She pushed her glasses up the bridge of her nose. "Beya, don't *do* that."

"Pardon, Milady." The housekeeper's gaze traveled the now well-organized room. "'Tis time someone took this room in hand, yes. An artist's touch it has well needed."

Annie's fingers itched to hold a paintbrush and bring one of the many empty canvases to life. "I can't wait to get started."

"But wait you shall." Beya, who was over a good two and a half feet shorter than Annie, reached up and patted her arm. "Dinner is served in your chambers and your creature is quite in need of companionship."

"Abra!" Annie wiped sweat from her forehead with the back of her hand. "Poor thing. More than likely she'll be giving me the silent treatment until tomorrow morning."

Beya smiled. "Come now. To your chambers." The housekeeper faded into sparkles, leaving Annie alone once again.

As she surveyed the room one last time, she propped her hands on her hips. Her arms, legs, and back ached, but she had that wonderful feeling of a job well done.

Annie gave a tired but satisfied smile in the direction of an empty canvas sitting on an easel. "Tomorrow you're mine, sugar."

Over the next few days, Annie threw herself into her art and pushed aside her nightly dreams. Every night she dreamed of leaving and finding her cousins safe and happy. The urge to leave and find the family who truly loved her grew greater every day, but she couldn't abandon Karn, not yet anyway.

When she first sat down in front of the easel, she hadn't known what she was going to create. Before she knew it she had fallen into an artistic trance, and when she came out of it the image of a man was on the canvas.

Her man.

Karn.

Daily, Annie poured her heart and soul into the painting, working on it until she felt it was as close to perfect as it was going to get. Since she normally did landscapes, it surprised her how well she'd captured the brooding, sexy look in his dark eyes as he looked to the distance, the fall of dark hair to his shoulders, the arrogant line of his jaw.

Annie loved everything about Karn, and it was breaking her heart to know she'd have to leave soon. She couldn't and wouldn't stay where she wasn't loved. It would slowly kill her to live with a man who refused to share his heart and soul with her.

From Aleana, Annie had managed to learn a bit here and there about her cousins, the Queen of Hearts and the Queen of Spades. The Kingdom of Hearts was the closest, several miles to the north of the Kingdom of Diamonds.

And she would leave now that she'd finished his portrait. It would be her final gift to Karn, a way of leaving her love with him, even if he didn't want it. Unconditional, no strings attached—pure and simple and colorful.

When she made the final stroke, a hint of shadow to the line of his jaw, her heart settled low in her belly. She was done. She could no longer put off the inevitable.

One more thing to do. Annie adjusted her glasses with one hand while she reached for a fine tipped brush with silver hair. Annie dipped the point into navy blue paint and then carefully signed the lower right corner.

> *To Karn with love,*
> *Annie Travis*

The incredible feeling of loneliness and emptiness that she'd forced back this whole week came crashing over her like the waves against the cliffs—pounding and pounding at her so hard that tears forced their way past her eyes and spilled onto her cheeks. With angry jerks of her hand, she swiped at them. Crying was useless, and she might as well get over him now. She was a big girl, and it was time to act like it.

After she cleaned the brushes and packed all the art supplies neatly away, she stood for a moment in the doorway, carefully holding Karn's portrait with one hand. The room's smells of almond-scented brush cleaner, oil paints, and cedar wood would be forever imprinted on her mind.

Annie closed the door, the heavy wood easily sliding shut with a click and a resounding thump. Taking care not to bump the portrait, she stole back to her own corridor. She paused in front of the weapons room, then set the painting down so that it was resting against the wall. She slipped into the room and grabbed the smaller of the leather packs, then retrieved one of the sheathed daggers she had seen on her initial exploration of this wing. Once she reached her destination, she would make sure the dagger and pack were sent back to Karn.

She slipped the dagger into the pack for now, then she slung the pack over her shoulder. She left the room, closing the door tightly behind her, then retrieved Karn's painting and hurried to his chambers. She'd only been inside once before, when she'd swiped his shirt to wear.

Annie almost cried when she walked into his chambers and the full force of all that was Karn flowed over her. His presence filled the room from his raw masculinity to his unique male musk. Like the man, the room was dark and foreboding, yet infused with personality.

Don't cry! she admonished herself. *Tears are useless.*

She set his portrait on one of the trunks in the room and leaned it up against the wall. After the portrait was settled, she slowly took off her collar and laid it on the trunk beside the painting. She felt so naked and lost without the collar, the symbolism of what it meant . . . that she had belonged to Karn.

Biting her lower lip to keep from crying, Annie moved to the trunk where Karn kept his clothing. She didn't want to take anything from Karn, but she couldn't very well travel the moors in nothing but a tunic. She knew his clothes would be too big, but maybe she could roll up each pant leg and tie a scarf or belt around the waist.

When she dug through his trunk, her fingers brushed

something familiar, and she almost cried out her relief.
Her jeans. By the time she'd dug everything out, she'd
discovered that all her clothing was there, buried beneath his belongings. Her own jeans and T-shirt.

He'd kept them.

What that meant, she didn't know, but if she was going to sneak out into the moors, it was good she'd have
her own clothing.

Annie hurried through the connecting doors into
the bedroom she'd used since arriving at Diamond Hall.
She'd spent many wonderful days with Karn, before the
sharing tea, but her nights had always been alone. In
her heart she knew it was his way of keeping some distance between them. Not allowing himself to come to
care too much for her. She understood what had dam-
aged his heart so much that he refused to love, and it
was impossible to get past that. He guarded his heart so
well nothing seemed to get past it.

Abra was sitting at her crystal bowl, eating her dinner, and Annie's heart squeezed. If it wasn't for her cat,
her days would have been so much harder to take.

The cat gave Annie a haughty look that said, *About
time you showed up,* and returned to eating. Annie smiled
and sat down at the table where her own dinner was laid
out.

When she finished eating, she dressed in her own
clothing, then strapped on the sheathed dagger. When
she caught sight of the nipple rings on her dresser, she
paused for a moment. The diamonds glittered in the

candlelight and she couldn't help but remember the times she'd worn them for Karn, when they were alone.

Swallowing down the lump in her throat, Annie withdrew the traveling cloak from the trunk and slipped it over her head, then pulled on the doeskin boots he had given her for the walk along the shore. After she stuffed the leftover piece of bread into her pocket, along with a piece of fruit, she put the pack over her shoulder. She scooped Abra up from off the bed and held the cat close beneath her cloak.

A sense of déjà vu swept over Annie, but she shook off the feeling and slipped out her bedroom door and quietly closed it behind her.

Karn guided his golden *jul* through the misty moors. The beast gave a low whinny, and Karn had to agree, it was not a good evening to be out and about. Yet he didn't mind the rain against his face or the chill wind seeping through the opening of his traveling cloak.

What did concern him were creatures that preyed on travelers who dared to cross the moors at night. It was not fully dark yet, but Karn kept his sword across his lap and his senses constantly on the alert. Fortunately, the *jul* also had keen senses and could easily work its way through the fog to avoid stepping into the boggy locations.

The only sounds in the moors were the creak of saddle leather and the soft *clip-clop* of the *jul*'s hooves.

Even the *rian* were quiet this night, not a chirp or a trill, which did not set well with Karn.

Nothing sets well with me these days.

He'd left his kingdom to meet in Hearts to strategize with his brothers, Jarronn, Ty, and Darronn. The trip to Hearts was two days long by *jul*-back, and at least three if one was to go on foot. But to travel the moors in such a manner was foolhardy indeed.

Karn knew he should have taken Annie, but he needed space and distance. Both Alice and Alexi had been furious with him, and he'd been sure to guard his bollocks before informing them that Annie was at Diamond Hall. In just days, along with their mates, the sisters would arrive in the Kingdom of Diamonds to reunite with Annie.

And to witness Karn's and Annie's joining as King and Queen.

He couldn't help but care for Annie. Her gentle ways, how she blushed so easily, her desire to please him, and how she so easily interacted with his people and truly appeared concerned with their welfare. His subjects were enamored with their future queen, and Karn had to admit that he was, too.

But love . . . no.

His gut twisted as he remembered the look on his kitten's face when she overheard him talking before the sharing tea. He did not like that he had hurt her, but what was done was done.

No matter that he cared for her, he would not allow himself the mistake of falling in love with her.

When Karn finally reached Diamond Hall, he left the *jul* with a stable hand and strode toward the mansion. A queer feeling settled in his gut, but he pushed it aside. Right now he needed to bury his cock in his woman, to fuck her again and again. He'd dreamed of sliding into her quim, of suckling her lovely nipples and tasting her folds and bringing her to orgasm after orgasm.

He hurried up the stairs and almost trampled Beya as he raced down the hallway. "Pardon," he said, never stopping in his desire to be with Annie.

"Sire," Beya said as he opened his mate's door. "I must—"

"Not now," he said in a curt tone and entered Annie's room.

She wasn't there.

Her warm vanilla scent still lingered, mixing with the smell of *ch'tok* logs burning in the hearth. But his senses told him something wasn't right.

Beya appeared beside him, but he ignored her and charged through the adjoining doors to his room. Immediately, he saw the portrait across the room, sitting on one of his clothing trunks, the back braced against the wall. Annie's collar lay on the trunk, beside the portrait.

His steps faltered as he walked toward the painting. When he reached it, he dropped to one knee. Time stood still in that sharp, clear moment while he couldn't take his gaze from the portrait. His chest ached with a fierce and sudden pain and his heart pounded against his ribs.

Annie's heart and soul were obvious in every stroke,

and in her signature. She had painted him whole and full of color . . . she had seen him in ways that only a woman who loved him could express. He rubbed at his chest to chase away the ache, the same chest that Annie had so lovingly captured in the painting. The savage yet faraway look to his eyes, the firm set of his jaw, the sense that he was coiled and ready to spring with a mighty roar.

Yet, in his eyes she had shown the caring that he tried to forever hide from anyone who knew him. The love buried just beneath the surface that he had always kept hidden.

He had managed to hide it from everyone . . . from everyone but Annie.

Thoughts of his mother and her art returned to him in wave after painful wave. It had meant the world to her. Every time she painted a human subject, it was only of the people dearest to her heart.

No matter that he had done all he could to keep Annie from falling in love with him, no matter that he had kept himself at a distance, she still loved him.

And even though she loved him, she had left him. Every fiber of his soul told him she was gone. She had taken the few pieces of her heart he hadn't broken with his pride-cursed arrogance, and she'd fled.

Annie had left him, his kingdom, his people, and the only truly safe place in all of Diamonds because he had refused to admit the truth.

And what is the truth, my son?

Karn heard his mother's even, melodic voice, ringing from his memory like a warm spring breeze. He had never been able to lie to her, and he wouldn't now, not even to her memory.

Especially not now, when an honest answer might be his only route to salvation.

The truth is, I love her.

The realization punched his gut harder than any enemy, stabbed him deeper than any blade. *For all my blustering and damned fool games, I love her. And somehow, I must tell her, and try to mend the gentle heart I broke.*

"She is gone, Sire." Beya's voice faltered. "Just as you arrived, I discovered it. I intended to set the guard out to find her."

"No." Karn picked up the collar Annie had abandoned beside the portrait and clenched it in his fist. He got to his feet, his jaw set with determination as he set the collar on his bureau. "I will find Annie. And I will bring her home."

CHAPTER TEN

Annie cuddled Abra beneath the traveling cloak as she made her way through the thick mist. She carried a torch she had "borrowed" from the steps down to the doorway leading to the ocean. After retrieving the torch, she had hurried back upstairs and slipped out the front door without being seen.

Phantom shapes appeared and disappeared in the fog, setting Annie on edge. She'd put away her glasses since they'd be useless in the rain, and the shadows were gloomy and foreboding.

The pack at her back hung heavy with food she'd taken from the kitchen, and the dagger strapped to her side made her feel like an Old West gunslinger. Except, of course, she didn't really know how to use the dagger, and likely she couldn't hurt a thing with it, but she felt better just having the weapon with her. No doubt it would be ideal for cutting chunks of cheese and apples.

At least the rain has let up. Mist dampened her cheeks and hair, reminding her of San Francisco weather. After wearing primarily miniscule sheer dresses over the past weeks, her jeans and T-shirt felt strange, uncomfortable even. Mud weighted down her doeskin boots.

Annie realized she actually missed padding barefoot through the mansion and wearing those next-to-nothing dresses. She even missed her collar.

For Karn. I loved wearing the dresses and collar for him. Even the nipple rings.

Just the thought of Karn made her heart ache, but she would not allow herself to regret a moment of her time with him. Even though he wouldn't or couldn't fall in love with her, their time together had been special and she would never forget him.

Likely she would never love another man.

From beneath the cloak Abra shifted and gave a muffled *"Mewl,"* as if telling Annie that she loved Karn, too.

Her steps slowed and she wondered if she was doing the right thing by leaving. Should she have stayed and accepted whatever piece of Karn's heart that he was willing to give?

Annie pushed thoughts of her former lover away to focus on her journey and locating her cousins. Once she found Alice and Alexi, her mind would be free of worry and she could make a decision about her future.

While she passed the outskirts of the village, the clang of the blacksmith's hammer rang out across the night. She caught the smell of fresh bread from the bakery, mixing with the salt and brine smell of the ocean. The ever-present sound of crashing waves was a discordant reminder of home, yet tonight it was not soothing like the ocean rimming San Francisco had always been to her. The closer she got to the cliffs, the louder the sound was, and the more unsettled she became.

To avoid as much of the moors as possible, Annie had decided to work her way northeast along the cliffs, and then alter her course so that she was heading toward Hearts. She'd learned a lot from Aleana over the past week, and felt confident that even on foot she would arrive in Hearts within three days.

When she reached the cliffs, Annie paused and peeked over the rim to the jagged rocks below. Waves crashed and pounded the shore over and over, a fierce battle of water and stone. Annie shivered and moved away from the cliff's edge.

She paused and stared at the warm and welcoming lights of the village.

It would be so easy to turn back.

Again she wondered why she hadn't waited until morning to set out, and again she couldn't answer the question. She had felt compelled to leave, as if everything depended on it. Her life, the twins' lives, *everything*.

A few sprinkles landed on Annie's head, her cheek, and even the tip of her nose. Soon, a steady drizzle drenched her hair all the way down her braid. All the parts of her body that were exposed outside the cloak were quickly soaked from the rain. A chill seeped into her skin that the cloak and Abra's warmth couldn't begin to dispel.

A chill that seemed beyond the cold of the rain, beyond the blast of frigid air rolling off the moors.

Annie stood as silently as possible, listening into the night, hearing only the sound of steady rain and the ocean. But every fiber of her being told her she wasn't alone.

Something else was out there.

Without a backward glance at Beya, Karn shifted into a tiger, opened his bedchamber doors with his magic, and bounded through to find his bride. His paws made no sound upon the tiled floor as he rushed through the mansion. Long before he reached the front doors, they swung open, and then slammed shut once he passed through.

His keen weretiger senses immediately caught a hint of Annie's vanilla scent and her woman's musk. Why hadn't he noticed it earlier? Likely he had been too absorbed in forcing back his feelings for his mate rather than facing them and acknowledging his love for her.

Her perfume grew stronger as he rushed through the moors, toward the cliffs. Familiar evening noises filtered through the misty night along with the ever-present roar of the ocean. Rain began to fall, masking Annie's scent only slightly.

But in the next moment a powerful stench invaded Karn's senses.

His gut twisted and he doubled his speed. The king *shelenna*! Night be damned, but of all the beasts that haunted the moors, it was by far the most dangerous.

It should not be out of its winter hibernation yet, not till spring.

By the skies, what woke it?

Karn neared the cliffs when he saw the hideous man-sized two-headed beast.

And Annie was only feet away from the king *shelenna*.

Trembling with intense fear, Annie dropped the torch on the wet ground. It continued to glow, lighting up the night and the hideous beast in front of her. The monster was at least seven feet tall and its two heads bobbed up and down in the rain, both shark-toothed maws open wide. Its six eyes burned a furious red and the fists of its four hands clenched and unclenched.

Annie fumbled with the dagger beneath her cloak and managed to jerk it out of its sheath. The beast's stench alone nearly drove her to her knees—a stench like rotten meat and a backed-up toilet.

As she gripped the dagger in her fist, her eyes locked with the beast's. Annie's entire body stiffened. All her muscles turned to ice, and even her thoughts seemed frozen. She was unable to move, unable to decide what to do. She clenched Abra tightly in one arm and gripped the dagger in her other hand. Her heart pounded in her ears and her body shook from the rush of adrenaline.

The beast put her in mind of Grendel, but she was no Beowulf.

At her back was the cliff with the tremendous drop to the rocky shore below. In front of her, the two-headed beast. To each side was the small clearing and then the moors beyond. If she darted to the left, would the monster lunge at her? Would she be better off waiting for the beast to reach her?

Abra squirmed, struggling to free herself from Annie's death grip. With a *"Yerowl!"* the cat broke loose, tore across the small clearing, and vanished into the grassy moors.

"Abra!" Annie shouted. A fresh wave of fear rushed through her for her feline friend.

The monster paused, now maybe ten feet away from Annie. Three of the beast's red eyes tracked the cat while the remaining three stayed focused on Annie.

Annie held up her dagger and braced her feet in the slippery mud. Likely she would meet her death now, but she wouldn't give up without a fight.

The monster took another step forward. The coppery taste of terror filled Annie's mouth, and despite the rain her skin flushed hot.

The beast roared so loudly that Annie almost dropped her dagger. Her ears rang and her knees went weak.

Earth rumbled beneath her feet as the monster charged.

Annie stumbled back a step, her dagger held out before her.

Suddenly, a flash of white tore in front of Annie and slammed into the beast.

Karn's fury was so intense that his vision blurred and turned to red. He lunged at the *shelenna*, throwing all his weight against the creature. The *shelenna* roared even as it crashed to the ground, landing flat on its back in the mud.

Its talons sliced through Karn's fur to his flesh. Karn's claws and teeth ripped into the *shelenna*, tearing through the beast's tough armorlike skin. Its four arms shoved Karn away, tossing the tiger into the moors. Karn landed on all four feet and threw himself at the creature that had regained its footing.

No matter Karn's fury, the *shelenna* was an opponent that would normally take several weretigers to bring down.

But Karn would never give up. He was determined to best this creature and save Annie.

Cold fear washed through Annie as she watched Karn battle the horrid beast. The torch lying on the ground clearly illuminated the two figures fighting and slashing at each other with their tremendous claws. She clenched her dagger, wanting to help Karn, but not knowing how.

She had no experience and she was more likely to hurt him than she would the monster he battled.

He's bleeding so much!

Sparkles filled the sky, so dazzling that Annie was nearly blinded by them.

The monster paused, squinting its six eyes against the brightness.

Karn tore into one of the beast's necks, the sound of ripping flesh almost causing Annie to vomit.

Blood spurted from the wound, bathing Karn's white fur in dark red. The beast's undamaged head shrieked as the first fell limp against the monster's huge chest. The remaining head dove for Karn's neck, and Karn barely dodged the jagged teeth.

At the same moment, Annie saw tiny figures charging through the rain, toward Karn and the monster, each one of the small people holding long spears and shouting out a shrill war cry.

Munchfolk!

Annie's relief was so great she almost dropped her dagger.

She recognized Derk and thought she saw Ront, Lia, and even Beya, but everything was an incredible blur of mud, fur, blood, fangs, scales, and spears. The sound of metal piercing flesh sickened her, yet all she truly cared about was that Karn would come out of this alive.

Mud and blood covered Karn and the Munchfolk as they fought, and Annie could do nothing but feel helpless as she watched them.

A body was flung aside by the monster. It hit the

ground and slid across the mud. The tiny man bounded back to his feet and charged toward the melee again. Two other bodies sailed through the air. One of the Munch-folk jumped up to rejoin the battle, but the other lay still.

Annie started to move toward the injured man.

Her path was blocked by a pure white tiger. Its fangs were bared and it crouched, ready to spring at Annie.

The *shelenna* was weakening. Fatigue and loss of blood hampered Karn's fighting abilities, but he wouldn't stop until the creature was done for, once and for all.

"Save your queen!" Derk shouted to Karn as he rammed his spear into the *shelenna* again and again.

Karn whirled away from the beast. His heart pounded nearly out of his chest as he saw a white tiger.

It had Annie backed up against the cliff's edge.

Mikaela!

The sister who had betrayed Karn and his brothers was now attempting to kill Annie by forcing her off the edge of the cliff.

NO! Karn shouted in thought-speak, trying to catch Mikaela's attention.

Her head swung toward him and she shifted, white fur to skin and black leather, from tiger to human form. In her hand she held a long black whip, the leather writhing like a snake upon the muddy ground. With her eyes focused on Karn, she snapped the whip at Annie, coming within inches of her.

"Why do you think I brought her here?" Mikaela

smirked and propped one hand on her hip. "With a mindspell I convinced her to leave this very night. And I woke the king *shelenna* from its winter nap to ensure her death."

Leave her be. Karn's paws slipped in the mud as he took a step forward and considered his options. He had to take care because he knew Mikaela's talent with the whip was great and she could easily send Annie to her death with a flick of her wrist. *Kill me if you must, but let Annie live.*

Mikaela shook her head. "It will be so simple to send her body to the rocks below."

A chill rippled over Karn's skin that was even colder than the rain pouring from the skies. He shifted into his man's form even as he moved another step toward Mikaela. His body was covered in mud, and his countless wounds bled freely, yet he barely felt them. From behind, the sounds of Munchfolk battling the *shelenna* continued to fill the night.

Karn's gaze focused entirely on Mikaela. He would beg for Annie's life, whatever it would take to save her. "Please do not do this, sister."

A blank look flashed across Mikaela's angular features, as though surprised that Karn had referred to her in a familiar way. But the look vanished, replaced by cold calculation. "I will kill her, *brother*. If only for the joy of seeing you in pain. Why should you have what I do not—you, one of the four who received all from our parents?"

"I miss you." The words escaped Karn before he had

a chance to consider them but he plunged ahead. "I miss the sister I once knew and loved."

Mikaela looked taken aback for a moment, but regained her composure in mere seconds. "That person no longer exists."

"You're wrong." Karn held out his hand. "She's still inside, in your soul. Please . . . do not damage it further by taking away the one woman I love with all my heart."

Annie's eyes widened and she lowered her dagger. "You love me, Karn?"

Mikaela raised her chin. "That is why she must die."

"Do you not recall how close we were?" Karn took another step toward Mikaela. "Remember how we played 'catch the monkey tail' in the jungle behind the castle? And when we used to filch pastries from the kitchen and eat them in the grand turret where we were not allowed? Before the fever. Before the misunderstandings, the fighting, the hatred."

"Those days are gone." Mikaela's expression shifted, as if she was struggling with some inner battle. "I intend to rule Tarok. All of you and your mates must be exterminated."

Karn clenched his fists and took another step closer. "This is not the real Mikaela speaking."

Her eyes flashed red and her face hardened. "This bitch must die. They all must die." She raised her whip and snapped it at Annie.

Annie felt the sting of leather as the whip wrapped around her waist. A quick yank and the whip pulled free, causing Annie to slip on the muddy ground. One foot met air and the next thing she knew the ground vanished beneath her.

"No!" Karn shouted, and lunged toward her.

As she fell, Annie clawed the slippery ground with one hand, digging her fingers into the wet soil. With her other, she drove the dagger in the ground. For a moment she stopped, clinging to the side of the cliff with her free hand and the dagger. Her feet flailed, trying to find purchase on the wet cliff side. But she was slipping. She couldn't hold on much longer.

"Annie!" Karn threw himself to the ground and grabbed Annie's hands just as the dagger slipped free. It flipped over her shoulder, through the air, and headed down to the jagged rocks below. "Hold on," he shouted as he grasped her wrists tightly and pulled.

But Mikaela was advancing on them, whip in hand. Just as she raised it to strike, a small black and white creature bolted across the clearing, its green eyes blazing. It was all but a blur, it happened so fast, as the creature clawed its way up Mikaela's leather pantsuit, straight for her face.

Abra!

Mikaela shrieked and raised her hands to push away the cat that clawed at her face and gave a loud *"Yerowl!"* as though it were the fiercest of tigers.

Karn yanked Annie's arms, pulling her up over the cliff's edge and onto the ground at the same moment Mikaela was fighting off Abra.

The woman shifted into a tiger and Abra tumbled

to the ground. Just as Mikaela was about to swipe a massive paw at the cat, her back legs slid in the mud and out from beneath her, right over the side of the cliff.

Annie was on her knees, ready to dive for her cat.

Mikaela slipped over the edge, her front tiger claws pawing at the ground. Karn threw himself toward Mikaela, reaching out to grab one of her paws.

But it was too late. Mikaela gave a loud roar, then vanished from sight.

Annie scooped Abra into her arms and buried her face in the cat's drenched fur. Everything was silent, outside the roar of the ocean and the sound of rain pounding the moors. Even the battle with the Munchfolk and the *shelenna* had gone quiet.

Slowly, Annie raised her head to see Karn on one knee, both hands over his face. He ran his palms upward, pushing his hair out of his eyes. "Maybe it is for the best," he said quietly. "Her soul has been tortured for far too long."

With a sob, Annie threw herself at Karn. He wrapped her in his arms, and Abra mewled at being caught between them. The cat slipped out of her grasp and landed gently on the ground as Karn brought Annie tighter into his embrace. They were on their knees in the rain, clinging to each other for a long moment and not saying a word.

Finally, Karn said, "I love you, Annie. With all my being, I love you."

Annie tilted her face up to look into his serious

midnight-black eyes. "The moment I saw you in the painting before you brought me here, you had my heart, Karn. It belongs to you, just as I do."

He kissed her then, soft and sweet. Annie tasted rain and mud and blood mixed in with his unique flavor. At that moment, she didn't care about anything but being in his arms and knowing that he loved her.

After Karn made sure his mate was unhurt, he forced himself toward the edge of the cliff. His heart ached for the sister he had known and loved so long ago. He would go down the path to the shore, recover Mikaela's body, and see to it that she received a proper Tarok burial.

But when he peered over the edge, nothing was there. Only ocean pounding rock and shore.

After the Munchfolk had buried the *shelenna* in the moors, they vanished in so many sparkles, taking their dead and wounded back to their homeland.

Despite Annie's protests, Karn insisted on carrying her to the mansion, even though he was wounded and covered in blood. With Abra in her arms, Annie snuggled into Karn's embrace, feeling a warmth in her heart and soul that chased away the chill from her drenched skin.

Without pausing to greet Beya who held the door open as if waiting for them, Karn strode up the staircase to Annie's chambers, and into the bathing room. The moment he set Annie down, Abra bounded from her arms, straight for Beya who appeared in the doorway in a burst of sparkles.

"Will you be needing anything, Sire?" she asked as she scooped up the cat. "If not, I will see to Mistress Abra."

Karn smiled. "Do care for that ferocious little beast." He turned his smile toward Annie. "I will see to this one."

Annie's heart swelled at the look in his eyes. He loved her . . . he truly loved her.

When Beya vanished with Abra, Karn and Annie stripped out of their clothing, climbed into the pool and, bathed each other. After they were clean, they toweled off and then moved to the bedroom.

Annie insisted that Karn had to sit on the stool in front of the mirror so that she could attend to the cuts and scrapes on his face and arms. In some ways, it amused her to have this big hulking warrior obeying her command.

With his magic Karn retrieved a Tarok version of a first-aid kit, and Annie followed his instructions on which pastes and gels to use on the wounds. The paste had the scent of mint and oranges, and was used to sterilize the wounds and to protect them from infection. The gel's odor was not particularly pleasant, like it had been made from a nasty-smelling ragweed. But the stuff was incredible because it was like a liquid bandage. The moment she rubbed it over a wound, it stopped bleeding and started healing.

While she treated his scratches, Annie's heart ached for every wound he had taken to defend her. "I'm sorry I ran away," she murmured as she dressed the last one.

She set the jar of gel on the dresser and knelt between his thighs. "I should have stayed."

Karn brushed her damp hair from her face and tucked it behind her ear. "It is I who should be sorry, kitten. You deserved to be showered with love, to be embraced and cared for. Trust me in that you have my love forever and always."

Annie reached up, put her arms around his neck, and pulled him down to meet her. "I know," she whispered, then kissed him.

He scooped her up in his arms and carried her through the doors to his bedroom, and he laid her on the bed. It was the first time she had ever been on his bed, and the tenderness in his eyes and in how his cared for her nearly brought tears to her eyes.

When he lay beside her, Karn stroked his finger between her breasts, down to her mound, and back up. "There is something I have not shared with you yet, kitten."

"What?" She gave him a teasing look. "Don't tell me. You're not really a weretiger, you're a wereleopard."

The corner of Karn's mouth curved in a grin that was so sexy Annie nearly lost her breath.

"No, love." He leaned down and kissed her forehead. "A weretiger can release a *tigri* pheromone when he mates. After a time, his partner will begin the transformation to become a weretiger, too."

Annie stared at him, both surprised and unsure how she felt about it. "Have you released the pheromone with me?"

He shook his head. "You would have known it if I had. It would cause you to become quite wild and animalistic with your desire to mate with me."

"Wild animal sex, huh?" Annie gave him an appraising look even though she wanted to smile at the thought. "And what else is there to this story?"

"The *tigri* pheromones would enable you to live a very long life, long enough that we would grow old together." He continued caressing Annie's belly with a light sensual stroke. "You would live nearly as long as our cubs will."

His cock felt like steel against her hip, distracting her, making it harder to think. She struggled to let her professor brain sort things out, first. "That first night we were together, when I asked you about contraceptives, you said that we would have to reach simultaneous climax to impregnate me."

"I would also have to release my seed and you would have to be in heat to become pregnant with my cubs," he reminded her. He trailed his finger lower, toward her mound. "But as far as the change, the few times I released the pheromone would not be enough to complete the transformation to make you a weretiger."

"Wow." Was it really so simple? "As a weretiger I would be able to shapeshift, like you do?"

Karn nodded. "But it must be your decision. I will never take your right to choose away from you again."

Annie smiled and reached down and wrapped her fingers around his cock. "I say, what are you waiting for?"

With a loud rumbling purr and a feral look to his

eyes, Karn moved so that he was between her thighs, his cock brushing her belly. A warm musk flowed over Annie and the next thing she knew her body was trembling with the intense desire to have him inside her and to have him *now*. She knew instantly that the musk was the pheromone that he had spoken of, and it made her wild for him.

"Take me, Karn." She grabbed his cock and shifted her hips so that he was at the entrance to her core, and tried to arch up so that she could impale herself on his length. He just stayed still with an infuriating smile. Annie reached up and pulled his head down to meet hers and she lightly bit at his bottom lip.

Karn growled, then loosed a roar that rippled through her body like a small orgasm. He thrust his cock inside her and she cried out at the pleasure it brought her. Annie squirmed and called out for him to ride her harder and faster. She needed more of him, needed all of him.

She loved the way the pheromones made her feel— wild and free. Everything that had ever restrained Annie in her life melted away to nothing. And as she shouted with her climax, Karn's roar joined her cry, making them as one.

CHAPTER ELEVEN

BUTTERFLIES WERE HAVING A HEYDAY IN Annie's belly. She was so nervous she kept breaking out in a cold sweat, and then flushing hot again. Today was her wedding day, and soon she would marry Karn and become the Queen of Diamonds.

Annie pushed her glasses up the bridge of her nose. She thought about not wearing them to the ceremony, but she wanted to see everything clearly. She wiped her sweaty palms on Karn's leather tunic that she was wearing for the moment, just because it smelled like him.

"You've come a long way, baby," she murmured as she trailed her fingers over the silky crimson gown lying on her bed. "From virgin to wanton woman, from college professor to queen, from no love to plenty. Not bad for a country gal from Tennessee."

Abra gave a little *"Meow"* of agreement from where she was stretched out on the window seat. Even though Annie had been sharing Karn's bed ever since the night she'd run away, she wanted to dress in the beautiful rose room.

And any minute now her cousins would arrive. Annie was so excited to see the twins, she could hardly wait. She pulled the leather tunic over her head and tossed it onto the bed before picking up the beautiful crimson gown. When she slipped it on, it felt deliciously silky as it slid over her large breasts, full hips, and thighs, all the way down to her toes.

Voices sounded on the other side of the doors to her room. Abra scampered off the window seat and dove beneath the bed.

The doors burst open. Alexi and Alice whirled into the room with cries of excitement and the next thing Annie knew she was being hugged to death by two people she loved more than anything in the world—make that the universe.

"I can't believe you're here," Alice said as she pulled away and wiped tears from her eyes with the back of her hand. "When Karn told us, I just couldn't believe it."

"He's been treating you right, hasn't he?" Alexi gave Annie a firm look. "If he hasn't been taking care of you, I'll take care of *him*."

"Yes, he treats me wonderfully, Madam Attorney." Annie laughed and couldn't stop smiling. "Karn is an incredible man, and I love him more than anything."

Alexi returned her smile. "All right, but if he gets out of line, just let me know."

"I can't believe it's been two years since I've seen you, Alice." Annie stepped back and studied her cousin. Alice looked absolutely stunning, not to mention more confident and happier than Annie had ever seen her before. Alice's white-blond hair hung in long loose waves over her shoulders and down her back, and her aqua eyes sparkled. She wore a dress of white that was so sheer Annie could see the diamond nipple chain beneath it, not to mention her cousin's bare mound. At her throat was an exquisite diamond collar with red hearts made of rubies.

With a shake of her head and a grin, Annie added, "Sugar, you look gorgeous, but you might as well be wearing nothing."

Alice gave a mischievous look. "In Hearts that's exactly what I wear. Nothing but my collar and nipple chain."

"You're kidding." Annie's cheeks heated at the thought. "I don't feel so bad with my sheer little mini-dresses."

She turned to Alexi and held her at arm's length. "Hold on, sweetie. Let me get a good look at you." Alexi sported a short, very daring dress made of supple leather that had straps crisscrossing her breasts, barely covering her nipples. Her skin had a healthy glow, her blue-green eyes were bright with happiness, and her auburn hair was swept back and up in a sexy style. She wore a white diamond collar that had spades along it made from black diamonds.

Annie shook her head and smiled. "You look like a warrior princess."

"Talk about transformations." Alexi propped her

hands on her hips as she studied Annie in turn. "I knew all you needed was to get laid."

Annie's face went hot, but she said, "That's one thing I can say you were right about."

Both her cousins laughed, and then for the next half hour or so, they all chatted while helping Annie prepare for her joining ceremony. Alice and Alexi made Annie sit on a chair away from the mirror while they fixed her hair and put light touches of makeup on her cheeks, lips, and eyes.

They each shared their eventful journeys into this magical wonderland, how they met their kings, and what had happened to them along the way as they each fell in love. Alice and Alexi also talked about their children and the trials and joys of being mothers. Alice now had two sets of twins, two boys and two girls, and Alexi was the mother of triplet boys. They had left their children with their nannies at the castle in Hearts, and both mothers missed them terribly. In a day or so, Annie and Karn would journey to Hearts to spend time with Alice and Alexi and their cubs.

The joy her cousins felt was evident in their eyes and in the way they talked about their husbands and children. Annie was pleased that her cousins were so happy. The only thing that kept this time from being perfect was that Awai wasn't there to share it with them.

When the sisters declared that Annie was ready, they led her to the room's full-length mirror. Annie's eyes widened as she stared at her reflection. Her hair was piled up on her head with ringlets falling down her back and over one shoulder. The crimson dress had been a gift from Beya, and it was absolutely gorgeous. It was a strapless affair that barely covered her breasts, and sheer enough that Annie could swear her nipples were visible. The dress was fitted at the waist, and the skirt flared out and dropped down past her knees.

"I feel like Cinderella," Annie said, nearly breathless with amazement. "You two and Beya are my fairy god-mothers."

"You're much prettier than Cinderella." Alice fussed with a ringlet, drawing it over Annie's shoulder so that it hung just above her breast. "It's time to meet your prince."

Annie started to put on her red collar, but the twins insisted she leave it in the bedroom.

The walk down the hall, then the stairs, and then to the back of the mansion seemed to take forever. But when they reached the red and gold stained-glass doors leading out to the garden, the butterflies in Annie's belly kicked into gear. Alice and Alexi each pushed a door open, allowing Annie to walk into the garden where the private ceremony was being held on the other side of the flower wall.

Birds chirped and the sun peeked through the cloudy sky. The breeze felt cool on Annie's bare shoulders and the roar of the ocean made a fine wedding march. The twins followed Annie, both silent now, as she approached the wall of brilliant red starflowers. The air smelled of their sweet perfume, mingling with the salt and brine of the ocean.

Annie paused for a moment, remembering the first time she went to Karn. This was where she lost her virginity, and where she and Karn had spent countless hours making love.

"I am so happy you're here in Tarok," Alice said, then kissed Annie's cheek and gave a teary smile before vanishing around the flower wall.

"You let me know if Karn doesn't treat you right." Alexi hugged Annie, then went around the wall to stand beside her king where the joining party waited.

With a deep breath, a smile, and absolutely no regrets, Annie rounded the wall of flowers to meet her man and her destiny.

Karn waited with anticipation for his future queen. He hadn't felt such pure joy since his childhood. With her sweet and gentle ways, and her unconditional love, Annie had freed his heart, and had given him the greatest of gifts.

The ability to love in return.

He ignored those in attendance, his impatience to join with his mate growing as he watched for her. They had kept the guests to the joining ceremony to a minimum, only inviting their closest family and friends.

Ty had his arm around Kalina's shoulders and Aleana perched on Lord Kir's lap. Karn had no doubt the quartet would be enjoying one another's pleasures as soon as the ceremony was over.

Alice came around the wall of flowers and slipped

onto Jarronn's lap, and Alexi joined Darronn. Lia, Derk, and Ront completed those in attendance.

Where is Beya?

When Annie finally appeared around the wall of flowers, Karn wasn't sure he would be able to take another breath. She was so beautiful and so perfect for him.

Karn's heart swelled with pride as he watched his mate move toward him. Annie's smile was radiant, her brown eyes warm with happiness as she walked down the red carpet laid out between the guests' chairs.

Annie thought Karn never looked as handsome as he did at that moment, even with the healing scratches along his arms, neck, and face from his battle with the *shelenna*. He wore a finely made black leather tunic and pants so snug they showed off his enormous bulge. A breeze stirred his dark hair about his neck, his head was held high and proud, and the fire in his dark eyes told her that he wanted nothing more than to take her away and make love to her for hours on end.

I can hardly wait.

By the time Annie reached Karn, her heart was racing and she was sure she wouldn't be able to speak a word.

Karn took both her hands in his. "My kitten," he started as he smiled down at her. "You are everything I could hope for in a mate, and more. You taught me how to love again. You gave wings to my heart and it soars for you."

Tears of happiness threatened to spill down Annie's

cheeks. "I love you," she said, her voice loud and clear. "You are my heart and soul."

Karn drew Annie into his strong embrace and kissed her, his lips gentle yet firm.

A murmur and a couple of snickers came from the crowd. Karn broke the kiss and they both turned to see Abra strolling down the red carpet, with her head high and a thick diamond collar around her that was so big on her little neck it dragged on the carpet. At the end of the aisle Beya stood beaming with pride.

When Abra reached them, Karn released Annie's hands. He bent over and slid the collar from the calico cat's head. "Thank you, Mistress Abra," he murmured as he stroked her under her chin.

Abra said *"Meow,"* and purred loudly, then turned away to rejoin Beya.

Annie had been watching the entire scene in amazement. When Karn straightened, he held the collar out on his palm. It was made from white diamonds with red diamond shapes along it, each shape made from red rubies. The collar sparkled in the sunshine and was so dazzling that Annie couldn't take her eyes from it.

"Will you wear my collar?" Karn's ebony eyes locked with Annie's. "No matter your choice, you are queen of my heart and soul, and you are the Queen of Diamonds."

Annie didn't think it was possible to be any happier than she was at that moment. That happiness welled up inside her. Unlike the quiet and reserved Annie Travis who had arrived in Diamonds, she flung her arms around Karn's neck and planted a kiss on his lips.

When she pulled away she smiled even bigger at the sexy grin on Karn's face. "Absolutely I'll wear your collar, Karn. I love you so much I'd do anything for you."

His pleasure at her response was evident in his dark eyes as he clasped the collar around her neck. The moment he finished, applause broke out from the wedding party.

Karn took Annie's hand and faced the small crowd. "I present you with the Queen of Diamonds."

More applause, and Annie could see tears in both Alice's and Alexi's eyes. Beya had a proud motherly look on her face as she held Abra in her arms. When the applause died down, Abra gave a loud *"Meow,"* which Annie took for the cat's approval.

As they walked hand in hand down the aisle, the guests showered them with red blooms that caught in Annie's hair.

Once they had left the guests and disappeared behind the starflower wall, Karn scooped Annie up in his arms, causing her to cry out with surprise. She slipped her arms around his neck and started kissing his jawline and nipped at his ear.

Karn gave a rumbling growl. "Do you wish for me to take you in this very garden, observers be damned?"

Annie laughed and kissed him. "You could take me anywhere you want, big guy."

He growled again, but he pushed through the stained-glass doors and headed through the mansion to the stairs. Annie swore he bounded up the steps faster than he could in tiger form and then took her to his bedchamber and slammed the door shut behind him.

His expression was so fierce and tigerly, yet he laid her on the bed like she was the finest porcelain doll. He eased onto the bed beside her and propped himself on one elbow while he gently stroked her cheek with his fingertips.

Karn could barely rein back the desire to slide into his mate and consummate their joining. "I want to make this day special for you, Annie. Tell me what you want from me." He trailed his fingers down her neck and over her diamond and ruby collar as he spoke. Pride filled him that she had accepted his gift. "I will give you all that I have and more. I would command the stars to shine brighter and the moon to glow a more brilliant gold."

"I have everything I want." Annie's sweet smile warmed his heart like nothing else could. "I have you." She reached up and gently brushed her fingers over one of the scratches on his face from the *shelenna*. "And right now I want you to make love to me."

"Your wish is my command, my Queen." Karn brushed his lips over Annie's. She shivered as he moved his mouth along her jawline and then down her neck to her collarbone. She smelled of warm vanilla, a scent that made him hungry for more of his woman.

"Maybe that's too slow," she murmured as he flicked his tongue over the curve of her breast.

Karn chuckled, enjoying giving his mate pleasure. "I wish for you to never forget our joining." He removed her glasses and set them on the table beside the bed.

"How could I?" Annie asked, then gasped as he pulled down the strapless bodice of her dress, exposing her large and beautiful breasts.

His lips found one nipple and he flicked his tongue over it while tweaking her other nipple with his thumb and forefinger. Annie moaned and arched up into his caress. She slipped her fingers into his hair and held on as she squirmed.

The feel of Karn's mouth on her body was so exquisite that Annie didn't think she could take much more without having his cock deep inside her. His mouth left her breast and he licked a trail down her stomach to her belly button. He flicked his tongue inside, causing wild sensations to skitter throughout her body.

He raised his head and drew her dress down, over her mound and thighs, then slipped it completely off and let it slide off the bed onto the floor. He returned to her belly and worked his way to her mound. When he breathed deep of her scent, Annie's cheeks heated.

"I cannot get enough of your woman's musk." He gently pushed her thighs apart and eased himself between her legs so that his face was just above her mound. "And your taste, it is like the finest of wines."

"Karn." Annie arched her hips. "Please, Sire. I can't wait."

He smiled, taking pleasure in Annie's wish to be dominated in the bedroom. "Spread your thighs wider, kitten."

She did as he bade, and his cock hardened even more.

Annie trembled as she waited for Karn's tongue upon her. But instead he nuzzled the curls of her mound then licked the insides of her thighs, his rough catlike tongue making her crazy. He would near her pussy lips, then back away again, causing her to whimper.

When he finally stroked his tongue over her clit, Annie almost came. "Sire, I'm so close now."

"Do not climax without my permission, kitten," he murmured as he thrust two fingers inside her core.

She whimpered as he moved his fingers in and out of her pussy and licked her folds, moving his tongue around taking her to the brink and back again, never quite allowing her close enough to reach orgasm.

"Tell me what you want," he said as he rose up, away from her pussy.

Annie needed her arms around him, to feel his weight upon her. "I want you inside of me."

"My fingers?" he said in a teasing tone.

Annie bit her lip then said, "Your-your cock."

He gave a soft laugh. "Say what you want me to do."

Annie squirmed. She was sure he meant the "f" word, and it was something she'd never been able to say out loud. "I want you to-to . . ." She hesitated for a moment then blurted out, "I want you to fuck me."

Karn growled and knelt between her thighs. With a wave of his hand, he spelled away his clothing so that he was entirely naked. "I will fuck you, my queen. But first I will make love to you."

Annie held out her arms, drawing him to her as he lowered himself. With one hand he moved his erection to her core and drove his cock inside her. She moaned at the feel of his huge cock stretching her, filling her.

She closed her eyes, but then Karn said, "Open your eyes, Annie. Watch me make love to you."

Without question she obeyed, and her eyes locked with his. Sweat glistened on his forehead as he slowly thrust in and out. The feel of him moving within her was almost more than she could take. Karn's unique masculine scent mingled with her woman's musk and his skin was hot and damp against hers. He kept his head up and watched her face.

"My sweet kitten," he murmured as she drew closer and closer to climax. "I love you so much, sometimes I think it is more than my heart can bear."

At his words Annie started to tremble, ready to tumble over the brink. Before she could beg him to let her reach climax, Karn said, "I want you to come now, Annie."

Orgasm flamed through her like fire licking her skin from head to toe. She felt her climax throbbing around his cock and felt it burn through her body in flash after flash of heat.

"Come for me, Karn," she demanded, her voice uneven. "I want you to come now."

With a tiger's roar Karn thrust once, then twice more, and shouted as he came. His cock pulsed inside her core and he pressed his hips tight against hers.

They rolled onto their sides, his cock still inside her, their bodies fused together.

"You're mine," Annie said with a smile. "All mine."

"You are a rare jewel, the most precious of gems," Karn said as he gently brushed her hair out of her face. "You are the greatest treasure in my kingdom, my Queen of Diamonds."

EPILOGUE

AWAI STEELE PACED THE LENGTH OF HER CON-
dominium, her heels sinking into the deep,
lush burgundy carpeting. She preferred not
to wear a bra and the silky material of her blouse rasped
her nipples, making them taut with hunger. Her short
skirt brushed her upper thighs and the star at her belly
button swung against her flat belly.

The condo smelled of carpet shampoo, pine cleaner,
and fresh paint. It was bare of all furnishings, everything
put into long-term storage.

Because tonight *they* would come for her.

Awai snapped her leather whip, the crack loud and
satisfying. It was exactly a year since Annie vanished,
two years for Alexi, and three years to the day that Alice
had disappeared.

Without a doubt Awai knew she was next.

"Let them come," she murmured and snapped her
whip again. She didn't know who had taken her nieces,

but whoever they were, they would pay dearly if the girls had come to any harm.

After Annie vanished, Awai spent the year preparing for today. The first thing she did was put all of Annie's belongings into storage with Alexi's and Alice's possessions. Then gradually throughout the year, Awai sold her advertising agency along with all her shares of stock, her condo, and her Mercedes SL600. Every penny Awai owned, totaling well over five million dollars, was in an account earmarked for a women's shelter that aided victims of domestic violence. If Awai didn't return within a specified amount of time, the funds would go to the shelter. Her estate and her nieces' belongings would be taken out of storage and given to the same facility.

Awai paused in her pacing and moved to the expansive window that stretched along two sides of the large common room. Her view of San Francisco was magnificent, and tonight was no exception. City lights glittered in the darkness and so did the lights along the Golden Gate Bridge. No doubt she would miss this view, wherever she was going, but she missed her nieces more. A constant ache had taken residence in her heart and soul, and she wouldn't rest until she found Annie, Alice, and Alexi.

Awai was only a few years older than her nieces, being their aunt by marriage. Long ago, she had married the girls' uncle, John Steele—

And the bastard had nearly killed her.

A hard and cold knot expanded in Awai's gut like it

did every time she thought of the asshole. She had been young, innocent, and fresh out of high school when she met John. He had wooed her with his charm and expensive gifts, and had seduced her into his bed.

Awai ran the leather strap of her whip over her palm as her thoughts turned back to that horrid time in her life and her triumph in making a new life for herself.

Once she escaped the bastard, she'd promised herself that no man would ever dominate her again.

Awai raised her chin, no longer seeing the city lights, but instead the light of her past. With her intelligence and drive, Awai had quickly worked her way to the top of her profession in the advertising business. Eventually, she had started her own firm, and it wasn't long before she was drawing in larger and larger accounts until her agency was one of the premier advertising firms in the state of California. She became known as a ballbuster, the woman with brass ovaries. She didn't take shit from any man, and her staff was populated almost exclusively with women.

She had also started an extensive training program in the domestic violence shelter. With Awai's financial backing, the center taught women the skills necessary to enter the workforce. Frequently, Awai hired women from the shelter to fill positions in her company such as receptionist or filing clerk. Gradually, as they learned the ropes, many of the women were trained in more demanding tasks and worked their way up through the advertising agency.

Awai shifted and lightly flicked her whip, allowing it

to curl like a sensuous caress around her bare legs. The leather straps wrapped around her ankles and calves. There was another side to her life that no one knew about outside of her niece Annie.

Almost every evening, Awai left her daily concerns and entered the world of BDSM as a Dominatrix.

Awai treated her submissives well, making sure they enjoyed the erotic play, and always keeping the relationships safe, sane, and consensual. She had chosen to become a Domme simply because she had made that promise to herself . . . that no man would dominate her again.

Yet, something was missing. She couldn't quite place her finger on it, but she didn't feel complete in her role as a Domme. The feelings confused the hell out of her because she was not used to uncertainty. Awai knew what she wanted in life and went after it with a vengeance. So why was her role as a Domme not entirely satisfying?

As if I wished to be the one tied up and at a Dom's mercy.

She shrugged away the errant thought. *What the hell's the matter with me?*

Awai moved away from the window, a sense of melancholy rolling over her. She was known as a take-charge dynamo, and these feelings of confusion were pissing her off. Yet, as she thought more and more about her roll as a Domme, and of her missing nieces, she felt both angry and brooding . . . and regretful.

Awai snapped her whip in the empty room, the crack of leather jarring her back into her role. *She* would take charge and let the bastards who stole her nieces know who was boss.

When will the bastards get here? she wondered as she stared at the front door. It was well after ten—only two hours left until midnight and then the anniversary of all her nieces' disappearances would have passed.

Awai frowned at the stately mahogany door. *Could I have been wrong?*

No. She wouldn't allow doubt to make her feel insecure. Everything in her gut told her that *they* would be coming for her, too.

Since there wasn't any furniture left in the condo, Awai moved to the wall beside the door. She slid down the wall until she was sitting on the plush burgundy carpeting, setting her whip beside her. Awai's short skirt hiked up to her waist and her thong pulled tight against her clit. It had been days since she'd had a fuck, and for some reason the last one hadn't been as fulfilling as she'd hoped.

A wild fantasy had gone through her mind as she'd had sex with her sub. A fantasy of riding a powerful man, his cock filling her pussy while another man slid his cock into her ass. And yet a third grabbed her by her hair and forced her to suck his cock. She was totally at their mercy while all three men fucked her.

At the memory of the fantasy, Awai couldn't help but slide one hand down to her pussy. As she visualized the scene again, she moved aside the thong and fingered her clit. With her free hand she pushed her blouse above her pert breasts, exposing her nipples to the cool air in the condo.

She started out with small circles around her clit, then thrust one finger into her pussy and spread her juices over her folds. Against her will, she found herself back in the fantasy of the three men. This time one of the men was eating her pussy while another one kissed her, and the third sucked her nipples.

The thought of three gorgeous men focused on her pleasure, and in turn her pleasuring them, sent Awai into orbit. Her orgasm came hard and fast and caused her to moan as ripple after ripple of her climax continued to flow through her until she came a second time.

After she slipped her hand from her thong and arranged her clothing a bit, Awai relaxed against the wall and closed her eyes. She brought her fingers to her nose and scented herself, wondering what it would be like to smell the come of three men all at once.

What's the matter with me? Why am I fantasizing about dominant men? I should think instead of the men I dominate.

But the men continued to haunt her. Awai sighed and sank deeper into her thoughts until she slipped into a deep but unsettling sleep.

A blond god of a man tied Awai's wrists together with a golden rope. It was snug, yet the rope didn't hurt or cut into her flesh. He slid his hands down her thighs and calves then bound her ankles together, too, with the same golden rope. When he finished, he lowered his head to the juncture of her thighs and in-

haled deeply, his long blond hair caressing her skin. He gave a satisfied purr, and Awai felt a tingle in her pussy and her panties grew wet.

She tried to wake, but felt drugged, as though her eyelids weighed several pounds.

Awai was a fighter. She struggled to open her eyes . . .

She jerked awake and found herself still positioned with her back to the wall. She blinked away the sleep, struggling to fight off the drugged feeling.

Golden light shone across the living-room carpet, yet through the windows she could still see San Francisco's sparkling nighttime view. Slowly, she turned her head and saw that the door was open . . . and sunshine was spilling into her home.

Her heart pounded like mad, and she tried to get to her feet, only to slide down the wall and fall onto her side, her cheek resting on the leather handle of her whip.

Her hands and ankles were bound, just like in her dream.

Awai's breathing was hard and fast as she glanced at the golden rope around her wrists and then looked to her ankles.

A shadow fell across the carpet.

Awai's gaze shot to the doorway and she saw the golden god from her dreams. His white-blond hair tumbled over his shoulders, his muscled chest was bare, his magnificent six-pack abs featured a tattoo of a club. Good lord but those leather pants cradled his impressive family jewels, and despite the fact that she was tied up and at his mercy, Awai's pussy tingled.

Instead of the diatribe she had planned when "they" came for her, Awai found herself absolutely speechless.

The golden god flexed his muscles as he moved closer and knelt before her on one knee. His intense green eyes focused on her and he smelled of sun-warmed flesh and mountain air. Gently, he brushed the back of his hand over her cheek, and in a voice that sent shivers down her spine, the god said, "I have come for you."

PLEASURE...
PASSION...
DESIRE...
OH MY!

Don't miss out on this very steamy...very sexy paranormal series!